GOING IT ALONE

Gilbert Averell avoids some of the rigours of taxation by living for part of each year in France – but he is unhappy about the number of weeks he spends away from his native country. So when his look-alike friend, Georges, suggests that they swap passports for a short spell, Gilbert seizes the opportunity. However, a number of incidents involving Gilbert's sister and nephew begin to suggest that Georges' offer was not made out of simple friendship...

GOING IT ALONE

GOING IT ALONE

by

Michael Innes

Dales Large Print Books
Long Preston, North Yorkshire,
BD23 4ND, England.

British Library Cataloguing in Publication Data.

Innes, Michael
    Going it alone.

    A catalogue record of this book is
    available from the British Library

    ISBN   978-1-84262-566-8 pbk

Published in Large Print 2007 by arrangement with
A P Watt Literary, Film & Television Agents

Dales Large Print is an imprint of Library Magna Books Ltd.

Printed and bound in Great Britain by
T.J. (International) Ltd., Cornwall, PL28 8RW

PART ONE

PARIS AND BOXES

1

There is a story to the effect that when Thomas Hardy's *Tess of the D'Urbervilles* was first translated into Japanese the novel had to be drastically abbreviated. Hardy's own understanding of this was customarily conveyed in the words, 'They like literary works to be very short'. But his wife – his second wife – put a different colouring on the matter. The Japanese, she would explain, hold it virtuous in a girl to sell herself to assist her family, so a substantial part of Tess' tragedy as her creator had conceived it would merely perplex the readership being aimed at in the particular market involved.

The present chronicle does not concern the seduction of any innocent country girl. Yet this fragment of literary history has its relevance for us, since it turns upon the fact that the canons of public morality can vary a good deal from quarter to quarter of the globe. It may even do so as between one and the other side of the English Channel. Of this the business of paying one's taxes is a signal instance, and it is here, as it happens, that we must begin.

There are countries in which (although it

seems very shocking to *us*) defrauding the tax-gatherer is held to be positively virtuous, just as Tess' resigning herself to living with the nasty Alec d'Urberville is credited with being in the eyes of Japanese citizens of the most unimpaired moral perception. In England, on the other hand, it is held far from proper to behave after this fashion, and we are admired by our friends (and commended by our accountant) only if we so dispose our affairs as 'not to attract' more taxation than we must. Here is a key phrase, indeed, in the vocabulary of many honourably prosperous and public-spirited and patriotic persons. If, for example, it is fiscally advantageous to make your permanent abode in Paris or Rome rather than in London nobody is going to think twice about asking you to dinner or, for that matter, taking you on as a son-in-law. And if you retain your British nationality you may even be awarded some signal honour by the Crown.

Gilbert Averell – with whom we shall have much to do – fell roughly within this category, although he can scarcely be held to have been characteristic of it. He wasn't a pop star. He wasn't a retired tycoon living on his loot. He might, indeed, have been held to belong with those described by the poet as loitering heirs of city directors, since he had been left – and was content to live upon the income from – a moderate fortune acquired by a father who had laboured in the City of London. Properly provided with a classical education, he had been at Cambridge in the flight that just misses a fellowship. He had never ceased to regret the failure, and it was his secret hope that he might one day be elected into an honorary fellowship at his old college. There was nothing presumptuous about this unconfessed ambition of Gilbert Averell's, since he had employed the leisure his private income allowed him in establishing himself as a private scholar of considerable distinction. His classical training had led him early in his career to the writing of a respectable monograph on the plays of Racine, and from this he had moved onto the field of Anglo-French literary relations. He made many friends in France – not only in the universities but in the higher reaches of society as well, since he possessed the perfect diffidence and unobtrusive reserve which the French fondly suppose still to characterize persons of birth and breeding in these islands.

Such circumstances might in themselves have disposed Averell to embrace something like an expatriate condition. But his doing so had undoubtedly been promoted by financial considerations also. He was a bachelor, but one possessed of sisters, nieces and nephews to whom he was deeply but not too obviously attached. And although the greater part of his

13

father's fortune had come to him absolutely he regarded himself as its guardian rather than as its sole proprietor, and he would have been distressed had he been obliged to feel that his devotion to unremunerative pursuits must operate gravely to the disadvantage of these relations. Here was where the tax-gatherer came in – or rather where, so far as was legally possible, he was to be bowed out. Averell was concerned a little to husband such wealth as he had. The necessary dispositions proved to be not too complicated. He established himself in the fair land of France. He came to England as often as he could and would then (unlike Shakespeare's princess) go well satisfied to France again.

Thus matters stood for a long time. Yet there was a limiting condition upon the acceptability of the situation. Averell came to feel that the British government wasn't over-generous in that number of weeks in the year he was allowed to spend as a guest in his native land. He came to feel there was something arbitrary and unreasonable about it; almost that here was a fiat or ukase that it would be legitimate to dodge from time to time if dodged it could be.

The only person in France to whom he confessed to this persuasion was his intimate the Prince de Silistrie. Georges and he were of an age, and so like one another physically that a stranger might have supposed them to be brothers. But in temperament they differed widely, and in this no doubt lay the basis of their appeal to one another. Georges, indeed, was himself something of a man of learning; he was very clever, and possessed of wide cultivation. Yet he was also rather wild – or at least possessed of a gay *insouciance* and aristocratic regardlessness which his more staid and circumspect friend was disposed to envy him. Georges judged the legal limitation under which Averell lay in regard to residence in England to be a mere *bêtise:* the sort of busybodyism that had disastrously entered the world with the *Code Napoléon.* This was a judgement not altogether fair in itself, since the drastic clear-up to which the French have intermittently given that name had been much desired by all sensible people even under the *ancien régime.* But no doubt it had heralded an age in which even persons of consequence are increasingly bossed around. Nevertheless it was incomprehensible to the Prince de Silistrie that his friend Gilbert's little disability couldn't be ironed away by a word in the right quarter. And at first he simply made a joke of the whole thing.

Then, one day, he turned serious – or as serious as it was given him to be. It was at the Polo, to which he had recently been elected, and he was entertaining his English friend to luncheon. Numerous august personages were sitting around, and their presence may a little have tempered Georges' customary exuberance.

'I suppose,' he asked soberly, 'it is a matter of the passport, my dear fellow?'

'That comes into it, certainly. I haven't really much thought about it.'

'But surely they just wave or nod you through? These things seem to be mere formalities. It is this comical EEC.'

'Well, not exactly. They know at once when I present my document that I am one whose date of entry or exit they must record. And then, I imagine, some routine inquiry is made.'

'But I have been told that you need have no passport at all. It is a unique privilege accorded you happy citizens of the land of the brave – or is it the bold? – and the free. Certainly of hope and glory, I recall. An Englishman needs no passport either to leave or to return to his own country. It is a marvel, that.'

'Not much more than a notional marvel, I expect. I certainly shouldn't get in before establishing that I am a citizen of the United Kingdom, or whatever the term is. So in the end it would come to the same thing. I'd be checked up on, all right.'

'But, my friend, if you entered regularly and then overstayed your parole, your ticket of leave. Would they clap you in the nick?'

The Prince de Silistrie was proud of his command of English idiom. 'Would it mean durance vile?'

'Oh, I think not. The only penalty would be in additional taxes to be paid.'

'Which would be vexatious, of course. What is your judgement of the claret in this curious place?'

'I'd not presume to offer one, Georges... It might be different if I were caught out in actual fraud. But that, you know, isn't my thing.'

'*En voilà une affaire!* Then it must be a yacht.'

'A yacht, Georges?'

'Always I have wanted to own a yacht. I shall buy a yacht, and learn to sail it. I shall hire a crew of Bretons, so admirably anxious as they are to break the law. Am I not *bretonnant* myself? On my mother's side, of course. We shall drop you in some secluded Cornish cove, and return later to pick you up. It will be like a taxi.'

'Georges, what nonsense!'

'Not at all. It will be friendship, and friendship is never nonsense. No, not ever!' The Prince de Silistrie had uttered these words vehemently, but now his brow clouded suddenly. 'Yet one must admit,' he said, 'that it is a little commonplace – yes? Such things happen, I am told, every day. And the commonplace is not your style, I

17

know.' He paused on this, but Gilbert Averell said nothing. He'd have supposed that the commonplace was his style. Except, he hoped, in his own field of scholarship and in a quiet way. He sipped his host's claret in silence. There was certainly nothing commonplace about it.

'He nothing common did or mean,' the Prince de Silistrie went on – presumably because he had been well crammed with English literature (and with everything else) at the Lycée Janson-de-Sailly in youth. 'We must think of something with more style. Something with a touch of *panache*. A vulgar term, but expressive in its way.'

Averell laughed at this – but restrainedly, since he had a sense that the Head of State himself might be sitting behind his left shoulder. His French was as perfect as an Englishman's can be, but he wasn't sure of ever having heard that *panache*, employed figuratively, was a vulgarism, although it was certainly trite. Georges was rather fond of instructing his friend in *nuances* of usage that he'd made up on the spot.

'Oh, I might have a shot at the really extravagant thing, my dear Georges!' As he said this, Averell was aware of it as a rash remark – or as a rash remark to offer to this particular companion. 'Once in a way,' he added, and was conscious that this didn't much mend matters.

'Then, my dear fellow, we must think along those lines, must we not?' As he said this, Georges smiled charmingly, and at the same time in what Averell was relieved to recognize as a dismissive fashion. And they talked of other things.

But the next morning Averell opened an envelope on his breakfast table and found it to contain, without an accompanying message of any kind, the French passport of the Prince de Silistrie. The futile little joke annoyed him, and he resolved to register his mild displeasure by returning the document at once. He shoved it in a pocket, went to the telephone, and called a cab.

'But it is so simple, so obvious,' Georges was saying to him half an hour later. 'And at the same time such a lark – and a practical joke, such as all Englishmen love. It is such fun pretending to be somebody else! I used to do it often as a boy. Sometimes for days on end. You could be now yourself and now me – day about, if it amused you. Even in French society you could pass as a Frenchman, if you were discreet. Or I think you could. The experiment would be an interesting one.'

'No doubt. Perhaps I might even call on your Ambassador in Kensington Palace Gardens.'

'Ah, that I could not advise. He is my uncle, you will recall. It might be awkward.'

'A lot of things might be awkward. If they questioned me at Heathrow–'

'But why should that happen, my dear Gilbert? The passport is in perfect order. And are we not like twins? Often I have heard people say so. It is a touching thing, that – to have a dear friend who is also as a blood-brother.'

'Georges, I'm simply not going to play.'

'But an Englishman always plays! He plays the game whenever it offers. It is a national trait such as all the world admires. And this game, of course, you need only play once.'

'I'd certainly not play it more often than that.'

Nine out of ten of Gilbert Averell's acquaintances would have declared that this was an extraordinary thing for him to say. The tenth might have recalled a young man in whom an occasional dash of high spirits had made itself evident from time to time, and who had even been known to enjoy getting the better of prefects, housemasters, deans, proctors and other vexatious authorities in divers elaborate and hazardous ways. Such impulses had never been frequent in him, but when they did erupt it could be powerfully for a time. And it is quite certain that he was now seeing the notion of making a little trip to England as the Prince de Silistrie in an attractive light; it would be amusing in itself, and it would prove to him that middle age was not yet carrying all before it in the heart of one almost habitually serious and retiring scholar.

'What about you while I was away?' he asked. 'Would you be me?'

'*Pourquoi pas, mon ami?*' Georges had clearly not thought of this, and was delighted at the discovery of a further absurdity in the affair. 'But not, perhaps in Paris – although it would be fun to try. Italy, shall we say? Your passport will involve no difficulties there. The eminent Mr Gilbert Averell will visit the little hill towns of Tuscany or Umbria, where disconcerting encounters are unlikely to take place. For a month, shall we say?'

'For a week.' Averell, who was being thoroughly weak, felt a reassuring firmness as he said this. 'And just once and never more.'

'Aha! Thus quoth the raven, did he not? *Allez-y!* And also *avanti!*'

'And *bonne chance* into the bargain.' It was a shade sombrely that Gilbert Averell thus bade a week's goodbye to good sense. For the moment, he was barely conscious that the freakish exploit with which he had landed himself was nothing more nor less than the perpetrating of a fraud upon the Inland Revenue. But he did acutely wonder whether any enjoyment was conceivably to be extracted from it. It would only make sense if prosecuted with *élan* – which was

21

another gallicism of the sort that the Prince de Silistrie was fond of making fun of. He'd have to try. To go through with it dismally would be too stupid for words.

2

Being driven back to his own apartment, Averell remembered a question one used to be asked in wartime. *Is your journey really necessary?* Just at the present moment, there was no doubt what his answer would have to be. He often had one or another specific reason for wanting to visit England, and was rationally annoyed that he was unable to do so without incurring some unacceptable financial penalty. But nothing of the sort was in question now, and what he had involved himself with was merely a petty act of symbolic defiance. Georges had been right, therefore, in saying that the thing must be done with style and with that plume, so to speak, waving. And this raised an issue he hadn't at all thought out. He was booked for a week's deception. But for how long was he booked for an act of impersonation as well?

It dawned on him that impersonation could be a deep and mysterious affair: one answering, perhaps, to needs and impulses wholly buried in the unconscious. Surely it must be something of this kind that had prompted him to fall in with Georges' bizarre and rather disreputable suggestion –

this quite as much, at least, as the attractiveness he remembered as attaching to mere undergraduate follies and pranks?

He would be turning himself into somebody else. Put thus starkly, it suddenly became an alarming idea. Clearly there were people who enjoyed doing just this – including, in a sense, the entire theatrical profession. And doesn't every child delight in dressing up? But all that was *play;* was imitation, *mimesis*, willing suspensions of disbelief. To plan veritably to foist an imposture on others was quite a different thing. Crooks of various kinds did it soberly – and probably joylessly – in the way of business. Crooks who got any pleasure out of it were to be found mainly in storybooks. Thomas Mann's Felix Krull, for instance: there, certainly, had been a chap with plenty of *élan* to bring to the job. But Gilbert Averell was no Felix Krull. (Nor was meant to be, the Prince de Silistrie might have added from his abundant store of English literary references.) Yet conceivably every Averell has a Krull inside him, hollering to be let out. Perhaps this was what had happened. And 'had happened' got it just right, since he knew quite positively, if mysteriously, that he was committed to the outrageous charade.

He had been seeing the element of full-scale, one hundred per cent impersonation as lasting for about thirty seconds at either end of the adventure: for just so long, in fact, as he was displaying that passport beneath a notice reading 'Other EEC Nationals', or something of the sort. He'd be himself in England.

He'd be himself in England – hiring a car at Heathrow (if he decided to fly rather than travel by rail and sea) and simply driving down to his elder sister's house in Berkshire. He'd have sent a telegram ahead of him, and his visit would occasion no surprise. His sister certainly kept no account of his regular English sojournings; it would never occur to her that anything irregular was afoot; the little visit would be the most normal, the pleasantest thing in the world. Then he'd return as he had arrived, and collect the proceeds of his wager. There hadn't of course been a wager. But the thing felt that way – and it was probably the best way to feel about it.

Yet all this precisely lacked the *panache* which would alone render the exploit other than feeble. He knew that he'd better keep it that way. The alternative was to sail (or tack or wallow) through a week in London as the Prince de Silistrie; to throw himself into the part for the benefit of porters and hotel clerks and waiters; to drop into French when some difficult English idiom appeared to elude him: every kind of nonsense of that sort. He found himself wishing that Georges *wasn't* a prince. To be a prince in France didn't mean all that. The younger sons of a *duc* – he vaguely seemed to recall – often perplexingly ran to the title of *prince*. But in England it sounded very grand. Something to be stared at.

Thus was Gilbert Averell still meditating when he got back to his own apartment in the rue Lafitte. And there a variety of small practical problems at once beset him. Was he to book himself out of France in his friend's name? There might be something slightly tricky about that. Was he to pocket a substantial sum in francs in the reasonable confidence that nobody was going to ask to see his wallet? If he did, and if he then changed them into pounds sterling even in small batches in England, would this involve his producing what purported to be Georges' signature? What about his suitcases, which were so boldly stamped *GA?* He knew that in all these minor matters there lay no substantial difficulty. They were harassing, all the same. He felt he wasn't really well cast in the role of adventurer.

Yet anything that added to the effect of challenge ought to be reckoned as a gain. The more of a pushover the thing was, the sillier would it be. He ought even to be looking forward to the sudden bobbing up of unexpected emergency, such as would require a quick wit to cope with. But what about the blankly not-to-be-coped-with sort? Suppose he fell gravely ill. Suppose he was knocked down by a bus. The game would be up – and not to the effect that he had simply been out-staying his ticket-of-leave. And it wouldn't be Gilbert Averell alone who was compromised. The Prince de Silistrie would be compromised as well. Georges would assuredly hasten to the land of the free (on that British passport, if need be) and grandly declare himself to have been responsible for the entire ludicrous and scandalous affair. They might both end up in what Georges called the nick. A magistrate at Bow Street or wherever might be amused, but was more likely to think of the Inland Revenue. It would all take – at the most optimistic estimate – a lot of living down. No betting man would give much for his chances of receiving that honorary fellowship.

For most of the morning he continued to confront the momentous issue (as it now seemed to him) of just how he was going to spend seven April days. Was it in London as the Prince de Silistrie; as an industrious hoaxer, in fact, building up a little fund of exploits with which to entertain Georges when he got back to Paris? Was it in London as nobody in particular, doing the theatres and concerts and galleries and whatever else offered by way of entertainment for a solitary visitor? Or was it as Gilbert Averell, visiting his sister Ruth Barcroft and her family in a perfectly normal way? Berkshire could be delightful at this time of year. There would be armies of daffodils in Ruth's wild garden, one day seemingly dashed for ever to the ground by a late frost, and the next erect again in brilliant sunshine. On the Ridgeway the winter's mud and rut would have dried out, and it would be terrain good for windy walking under scurrying cloud, a protean sky.

But about this attractive picture there was a snag. It was all very well to say that the visit would be perfectly normal; that no thought to the contrary would enter his sister's head. It wouldn't be normal, but part of a situation which, although merely amusing in Georges' eyes (and intermittently in his own), would perplex and distress Ruth were she to get wind of it. And Ruth, he very well understood, had endured her share of family troubles. It would be a great shame if her reliable brother Gilbert proved to have turned up on her as the consequence of what she might read as downright dishonest behaviour.

Faced with this sobering discovery, Gilbert Averell ought, of course, to have washed out the whole thing. But that, he thought, would be to represent himself to his friend Georges in a poor-spirited light; would even, in an irrational way, be a kind of hauling down the flag. No, he'd go ahead! But he'd opt for London.

This was Averell's state of mind (if mind it can be called) when his telephone rang. And it proved to be his sister on the line.

Ruth's voice came across with the complete clarity that long-distance calls so frequently achieve. She might have suddenly been in the room with him, so that the smallest inflexion or change of tone coming through the instrument seemed to carry a visual impression too – as of a smile, a questioning glance, a shade of perplexity or surprise passing over her face.

'Gilbert, it's Ruth. How are you?'

'Fine, only rather idle. How about yourself?'

'Not too bad. Do you hate the telephone?'

'No, of course not. Or not if it's you. Why?'

'You sound as if you're not being idle at all, but rather busy or preoccupied or something, and not terribly wanting to be disturbed.'

'Absolutely not. I've just been thinking about you, as a matter of fact. It must be telepathic as well as telephonic. How are all the family?'

'Just as they should be. For the most part.'

'Yes?'

'Gilbert, I don't want to badger you, if you're absorbed in things. I meant to write, but then I thought I'd ring up. This instrument's more revealing than a carefully composed letter, don't you think?'

'Perhaps.' Averell, as a scholar, had faith in the written word. 'But I've known it to generate misconceptions at times.' He hesitated for a moment. It was clear to him that Ruth was upset. And she wasn't one from whom small upsets elicited hasty appeals. 'Go on,' he said.

'I've just been wondering whether you might be coming home for a bit in the near future. But for God's sake don't think I'm trying to summon you. I know about that tiresome tax business, for one thing.'

'Oh, that!'

Hearing his own dismissive note, Averell realized he had taken a first step in deception within the family. It didn't feel at all nice. And if there was real trouble in what he sometimes facetiously called darkest Berkshire he ought not to be importing fibs into it. He knew the right thing. He must recover his own passport from Georges at once, and travel openly to England by the first available flight. It was something he'd had to do once before – on an overdraft at the ticket-of-leave bank, so to speak. It was simply necessary to notify some authority or other in writing, and everything became perfectly regular. If Ruth was in some substantial difficulty he'd do precisely this.

'Never mind about that,' he said, and this

time didn't hesitate. 'Is it Tim?'

'Well, yes – it is, rather.' There was a pause. 'Gilbert, I do need your advice.'

'Listen, Ruth – and what I say is absolutely true.' Fleetingly, Averell registered that this was an odd thing to have to say to a sister. 'I'm on the point of coming over, as a matter of fact. And I'll make for Boxes straight away.'

Boxes was the odd name of Ruth Barcroft's house.

'That's just wonderful.'

'Is there anything more you want to tell me now?'

'Yes. Or I don't know. Gilbert, do people listen in on these calls?'

'Good heavens, no! It would take an army to monitor cross-Channel chit-chat.' For the first time, Averell was really alarmed. 'So go ahead. Whatever it is, I can think it over in the air.'

'I think I'd rather wait, after all. It's silly. But I'm as nervous as a cat.'

'Very well. And now I'll ring off. There's just one arrangement I have to make in a bit of a hurry, as a matter of fact. I'll send a telegram about when I arrive. Keep going, Ruth. Goodbye.'

As Averell put down the receiver he noticed that his hand was trembling. But he made his vital call at once. It was to be told that the Prince de Silistrie was not at home.

31

In fact the Prince de Silistrie had gone abroad. And no, he had given no forwarding address – saying merely that he would be away for only a week.

So Georges had wasted no time. And it was up to Averell to waste no time either. He called the airline, and booked a flight in Georges' name. He'd enter into the deception in style, he told himself – even solemnly appearing to set out from his friend's deserted apartment.

3

Timothy Barcroft was twenty-two, and at twenty had experienced brief fame or notoriety. As a student he had come to hold strong views on the evils of capitalist society, nuclear weapons, sub-human housing, racialism, the CIA, and numerous other conditions and institutions that ought simply not to be. His condemnations and indignations tended to be on the sweeping side, and he was at various times a nuisance to sundry authorities with whom he came in conflict. Much of this happened because he was a very nice young man; and it was one of his chronic troubles, even grievances, that many, although by no means all, of his elected Aunt Sallys persisted in so regarding him even after he had taken a good hard swipe at them. He felt he wasn't being treated seriously – which is an unforgivable offence against the sensibilities of the generous young.

Then a day came upon which Tim was involved in a 'demo' that went wrong. It was to be as orderly as nearly all such manifestations are meant to be. But there was a rival 'demo' around; the police failed to maintain their planned *cordon sanitaire* between the two; and a vicious punch-up was the result. Tim found himself in court, charged with having picked up a labourer's shovel and hit a constable on the head with it. A good deal of very confident evidence was produced in support of this alarming accusation. Tim was remanded in custody; granted legal aid; that sort of thing. Then a press photographer came forward in his defence – happily possessed of a film (which had just escaped being confiscated) in which the doing of the deed was plain to see, as was – incontrovertibly – Tim himself, peacefully arguing with another minion of the law half a dozen yards away. So Tim was acquitted, and at the same time lectured by the beak on the hazardousness of associating with unruly persons neglectful of the right and proper ways of effecting beneficent social change within a true democracy. And a rather senior policeman called on him and made a strictly off-the-record apology for the unfortunate mistake that had occurred. Tim seemed to take all this well, and went his ways as before. There was a certain hardening in him, all the same, which occasioned anxiety in his family.

Gilbert Averell (or the Prince de Silistrie) turned these matters over in his mind while high in air above the English Channel. He felt that he had never done his duty by his nephew Tim, and this even although he was much attached to the boy. Or it might be better to say that he had failed in his duty to the Barcrofts as a whole. Ruth had been divorced, very much without fault of her own, when Tim had been quite small and the twin girls barely out of their cots. She was a competent and courageous woman, and a little older than he was. Nevertheless, he ought to have made her feel, much more than he had done, that he was prepared, as her only brother, to act at need as the head of the family. But that wasn't quite right, since he had always been ready, as now, to step forward in a crisis. It was steady background support, constant interest, that he had failed to provide. And what had been his real motive in long ago taking himself off to live in France? There would be more money for the Barcrofts one day as a result, but hadn't he packed up partly because family responsibilities bored him; because of this and because some very commonplace pleasures (which had in fact never much commanded him) were available with less fuss and complication in an expatriate station? Whatever his reasons, the thing had been second-rate in itself – just like this wretched joke to which Georges had persuaded him.

Of course there was no secure reason for supposing that, had he stayed put, he'd have proved any sort of good angel either to Ruth and her family or to anybody else. Tim, for instance: if he'd fussed over Tim when the boy was, say, in rebellion against a housemaster (or running after a housemaid) the effect might just have been to mess the boy up. And Tim wasn't a mess, even if messes were things he sometimes got into. Averell blamed himself, all the same.

Averell was sunk in these unsatisfactory musings when a man sitting next to him offered some commonplace remark about the flight. He did so in French. As they were travelling by Air France, and as Averell had shortly before spoken in French when buying himself a drink, this was natural enough. What was odd was that he replied spontaneously in English. Or it appeared, at least, odd to himself, French having been for so many years the language he employed more often than not. There seemed to be no particular reason why the stranger (who was a middle-aged and unmemorable little man of the clerkly sort) should be struck by this small linguistic circumstance, since an Englishman often enough essays replying in his own tongue to a speech in another the gist of which he has just understood. In Averell, of course, the mechanism had been different. Far from living his way into his part, he was becoming progressively more and more uneasy at the impersonation he had undertaken, and he had instinctively shied away from Georges' language. The stranger, however, did seem surprised and (what was surely perplexing) even a little amused. Averell remembered that the fellow had been close behind him as they had gone through the control at the airport, so perhaps he'd had a glimpse of that confounded French passport. That might be it. Averell, as he hit upon this explanation, was conscious of a kind of forward vista of such minute vexatious occasions.

'The name's Flaubert,' the stranger said, easily and in English. And he momentarily elevated above his head a foolishly under-sized porkpie hat.

Averell detested unknown persons who thrust their identity upon one with some such aggressive and underbred formula as this. Moreover, the name that the stranger had announced somehow added to the offence. There was no reason why a man encountered on an aeroplane should not be called Flaubert. There must be Flauberts around, although he couldn't recall ever having actually met one.

'Monsieur *Gustave* Flaubert?' he heard himself say.

This silly little irony was a mistake. Flaubert was delighted, and clearly regarded an intimacy as having been established.

'That's right,' he said, and much as if he were a celebrity who might expect to be thus at once identified. 'My mother hailed from Hull,' he announced. 'But my father was a provision merchant in Passy. *Alimentation générale*, as you may have heard us call it in France.'

'Ah, yes.' Averell found himself a little disturbed by these unassuming claims, or rather by the manner in which they had been offered to him – its implication being that he was himself an Englishman. He had told himself that occasions would arise in which a quick-witted response would be required of him, and perhaps this was one of them already. What if this intolerably familiar little bourgeois now blankly asked him for his own name? Was he to reply with *hauteur*, 'Monsieur de Silistrie', or was he simply to say, 'Gilbert Averell'? It would be possible, of course, simply to remain silent. A thrusting chap like this must be accustomed to being snubbed often enough.

But this particular small crisis (if indeed it was that) didn't occur. Flaubert was more interested in Flaubert than in his interlocutor.

'I've always been grateful to my mother for talking English to me,' he pursued. 'There's a great advantage in possessing the two languages, as I fancy you do yourself. In the commercial world, that is. If two languages come to you for free, as it were, it's not too hard picking up bits and pieces of a couple of others. And with that you're quite off the ground. They feel they can send you anywhere.' Flaubert paused on this, and to a disturbing effect of consulting a not too rapidly operating imagination. 'I travel in containers,' he then pronounced.

'In containers?' Averell repeated, perplexed. The image of a packaged Flaubert thus presented took a little sorting out.

'Advanced collapsible containers. It's a very strong line. Pretty well does away with having to fix up return loads. Any chance of interesting you, by the way?'

'I'm afraid not.' Averell had provided himself for his flight with the current *Revue des deux Mondes,* but hadn't in fact opened it – perhaps because its title was tiresomely symbolic of his own present predicament. He'd better open it now. The engines had changed their note, which meant the plane was beginning to descend. He'd have reached the safety of Heathrow (if it was safety) in no time. There, it oughtn't to be too difficult to brush this burr-like person off. Meanwhile, however, the conversable Flaubert ignored the respectable journal which his victim had brought up pretty well to his own nose.

'But this isn't a business trip with me,' Flaubert went on. 'Or not altogether. Of course one combines business and pleasure when one can. I keep up with my English relations, you see. You never know when people may be useful to you. That's a motto of mine.'

'I don't doubt it is.' The frigidity with which Averell uttered this gave him courage, and he lowered his *Revue* sufficiently to enable him to tap its open page. 'But you will forgive me, sir. I have to make a note or two on something here before reaching my destination.'

'London, is it?'

'No, not London.'

'Ah.' Fleetingly, Flaubert gave the impression of a rather stupid man surprised once more. 'Well, it's not London for me either,' he said – almost aggressively, Averell thought.

At this moment the little lights went on, and a young woman sternly called for an extinguishing of cigarettes and the fastening of seatbelts. Gilbert Averell breathed a sigh of relief. Release was at hand.

4

Most of the passengers were French, so there was quite a queue at the little booth labelled 'Other EEC'. Averell vaguely wondered whether they had names like Balzac and Proust and Malraux. Apart from this, names, strangely enough, weren't worrying him. He was scarcely aware that he himself *had* a name. It was as if, at this crucial juncture, some process of mild dissociation had set in. It was as if he were going through a trivial formality and there was nothing more to it. Georges' passport said 'Prince', since the Republic preserves the courtesies in these matters. But the man at the desk was neither impressed nor interested. It was only to be observed that he put a date-stamp on the passports of everybody coming in this way.

Averell was aware of a certain impatience in himself as he waited for his suitcase to appear on the appropriate roundabout from which he would have to grab it and trundle it through Customs. But this wasn't because he was afraid of the passport official having intuitive second thoughts and coming pounding after him. It was merely because he wanted to be well ahead of the vexatious Flaubert at the curious game of snatch-when-you-can that the contrivance imposed – distinguishably to the discomfort of the older and less agile travellers. Some of the more practised of these had secured porters with waiting trolleys, and had only to point with a magistral umbrella at their own particular gyrating property. Younger people stood poised in athletic postures, rather in the manner of fielders in a cricket match alert for the ball. It was a set-up calculated to impress upon persons like himself in their mid-fifties that they possessed neither youth nor age but only an uncomfortable hover-ing-point between the two. But when the moment came he proved comfortingly nippy, even retrieving a bulky bag for an agitated old lady beside him in the same instant that he ambidextrously secured his own possessions. It then only remained to decide whether he was Red or Green; the bearer or not the bearer of dutiable articles. Of course he was Green for all normal purposes. But what about all those francs? Suppose the officials on the Red side of the hall decided to do a spot-check on him, and he had to divulge this particular possession? They probably wouldn't be interested, since it was no business of theirs to control any petty flow of currency out of France. Only it wasn't altogether easy, in his present position, to think clearly about such matters. One felt one never knew. It was with considerable relief that he found himself over this last hurdle, coasting down a ramp, and then actually in open air. For a whole blessed week he was incontestably Gilbert Averell again.

There was the bus that would take you into London, the bus that would take you to the railway station at Reading, taxis and hire-cars that would take you wherever you wanted to go. With these last an element of bargaining was prudent, but Averell knew he wouldn't much bother himself about it. He was conscious of a sudden alteration in his whole nervous tone; of a buoyancy as if the very atmosphere had changed. The silly part of the affair was behind him. In front of him was a responsible mission, one vindicating his concern as a conscientious family man.

In this fond persuasion he was giving brisk instructions to a chauffeur when, as with the dreaded voice of Demogorgon, Gustave Flaubert spoke from immediately behind him. Averell, who had supposed himself to have shaken off this pestilent (and obscurely threatening) character, was a good deal discomposed.

'Did I hear you say Faringdon?' Flaubert asked, not at all in the tone of one who apologizes for eavesdropping. 'I'm going not far from there myself. We'll share this car.'

But for the declarative form into which Flaubert had cast what was not in itself a wholly inadmissible proposal, Averell might have contrived to turn it down in terms of reasonable civility. As it was, he was much more forthright.

'We will certainly do no such thing,' he said. And he jumped into the back of the car and slammed the door to. 'Drive on!' he said (or, rather, loudly exclaimed). 'Pay no attention to the fellow. He's a well-known nuisance, and almost always drunk.' And feeling the need further to emphasize these instructions and prevarications, he waved a hand violently in the air. The car moved off at once, its driver evidently having no inclination to inquire into the rights and wrongs of the matter. Averell swung round and glanced through the back window in time to see Flaubert apparently in urgent colloquy with the driver of another car. Then, first, the twists and turns, and then the long tunnel, which extricate one from the heart of Heathrow were blessedly behind him, and he was being projected at a steady seventy miles an hour down the M4.

He addressed himself to reviewing the family situation at Boxes as he was likely to find it. At this time of year Ruth would be getting busier in her garden every day. It would be among the vegetables for the most part. Ruth was passionately fond of flowers and had great skill with them. But of recent years she had persuaded herself – and tried to persuade her three children – that self-sufficiency must now be the prime concern of the small rural gentry among whom she had spent almost her entire life so far. The Barcrofts must be prepared to live entirely off the land, consuming nothing that they didn't themselves produce. That was why there were Chinese geese on the lawns at the back of the house and a couple of goats tethered now here and now there at the front. It was why the old stable had been turned over to half a dozen pigs and there was a perpetual cackle of poultry just beyond the orchard. It was why a hand-pump of the semi-rotary sort had been installed to draw up water from the slender stream that wandered uncertainly through the place. It accounted for the fact that family locomotion was achieved by pony and trap, and that it was by this conveyance that his sister made her way to the nearby small town several times a week for the purpose of picking up a rudimentary knowledge of various useful but entirely boring crafts through the instrumentality of evening classes.

There was nothing dippy about all this, and no levelheaded person would think of describing Ruth Barcroft as a crank.

Although she had acquired a good deal of knowledge about how fiendish chemicals make their way from sacks to soil, from soil to crops, and from crops to shops and then into the human stomach, she didn't believe that we were all soon going to sprout extra toes and disastrous mental aberrations. She didn't, so far as her brother knew, devour apocalyptic science fictions or get hung up on television serials in which isolated handfuls of handsome young men and sexy girls struggle for survival amid the ruins of a civilized world. She just believed in a rapidly disintegrating society in which one would have to look out for one's self and one's children and grandchildren (not that she herself had any grandchildren as yet). Ruth's activities, in fact, were all within the bounds of good sense.

In much of this Tim Barcroft must be thought of as his mother's child. He held the same views on how things were going to work out, in his generation if not in hers. Tim's, however, was in a way a more masculine response. Where his mother was intent simply on preserving the home and the hearth he was all for going out and taking a bash. Tim was a political animal – the leader of a pack, say – in the making, and might be an effective one if given his chance. At the moment Tim was no more than a confused Oxford undergraduate, who had hung on to his studies because he contrived to see some of them as in some way 'relevant' to the social predicament which clamoured to be sorted out. Tim – Averell remembered forebodingly – wasn't an easy youth for a dim scholar to keep on terms with. He was always polite, even friendly, almost affectionate at times in an indulgent way. But the total 'irrelevance' of his uncle's pursuits was all too patently clear to him. He'd be at home at present, it was to be supposed, unless he was spending his last Easter vacation before his finals in mugging up some necessary lore elsewhere. It wasn't improbable that he was working hard, since his mother's good sense was far from alien to him, and he knew he'd been largely wasting his time over the past three years if he wasn't now preparing for what he'd call jumping through their bloody paper hoops.

The twin girls, Kate and Gillian, were younger, and Averell felt he didn't know as much about them as he ought to. Was it with reluctant feet that they were standing where the brook and river meet – or were they all for plunging in? Certainly they were at the very end of their schooldays, and both were said to be quite clever. Clever enough to go up to Oxford themselves, if their mother's letters were to be believed. They would have to decide, it seemed, whether to have a go at a college gone 'co-residential' in the newfangled way (their uncle thought of it as that) or to one still as conventual as the academe Lord Tennyson lost his nerve about. It comforted Averell to remember that for some years he'd been tipping permitted sums into a trust fund designed to pay for whatever variety of higher education these young people elected.

The car had turned off the motorway and was running through Lambourn, and quite soon he would see the line of the downs beneath which Boxes lay. It was a countryside speaking to him of his childhood, and he was indulging in melancholy thoughts of his elected condition of exile as the car swung round on the road to Wantage. It wasn't the shortest route, and he was about to call out something to his driver when, rather surprisingly, he discovered in himself a feeling that he might usefully employ an extra ten minutes of solitude in clarifying his mind. As he didn't know the situation in his sister's household he couldn't work out the right line to take about that, but the point was that he hadn't quite discovered what was the right line to take about himself. Stretching the term a little, he was nothing less than a fugitive from justice, and it seemed an abuse of hospitality to park himself on Ruth without declaring the fact. This was a notion distinctly on the quixotic side, but it genuinely worried him, all the same. So he must *think*.

But he didn't. When he found himself in traffic badly snarled up in Wantage market place, and the driver had resignedly switched off his engine, Averell took the opportunity to nip out and buy himself a morning paper. In Paris he regularly received *The Times*, but didn't always so much as glance at it. Now he found himself dodging his present obscure mission by burying his nose in a paper of a more popular cast.

It afforded a gloomy survey of events alike at home and abroad. Unspeakable things were happening in several parts of Africa. There was political chaos in Spain. Rioting on a large scale had erupted in Rome. In the industrial Midlands all sorts of people were on strike, and all sorts of other people unable to work as a consequence. Ireland was in as much of a mess as it had ever been in Mr Gladstone's time. Desperate criminals were being pursued down motorways such as he had himself just traversed by police cars constrained to travel at a hundred miles an hour. The younger members of the aristocracy were being had up for indulging in the same turn of speed just for fun. Demotic singers and pop groups went around apparently dripping undesirable drugs. Kidnappings for ransom and the snatching of hostages for no clear purpose at all seemed to be on a daily up-and-up. And on the credit side the ledger didn't read too cheerfully either. A group of economists of a sanguine turn of mind were predicting a conceivable improvement in the nation's affairs at some date in the earlier 1990s. Scotland Yard was being congratulated on having brought down the total of major bank raids to single figures in the month of March.

Oh world, no world, but mass of public wrongs, confused and filled with murder and misdeeds! Old Thomas Kyd's gloomy character would certainly reiterate this imprecation with spirit were he alive today. And it was the world, Gilbert Averell told himself, that Tim and Kate and Gillian would perhaps have to confront for the rest of their lives. Perhaps their mother was right in striving to build her little citadel.

The buoyancy that had attended his release from Heathrow had decidedly evaporated. The car turned into the potholed drive to Boxes.

5

Nobody knew how Boxes had come by its name. It was not box-like in any way but large and rambling, and with gardens (now sketchily cared for) which would appropriately have gone with a house larger still. Ruth had bought it at the time of the break-up of her marriage, putting much of her available means into it even although she had got it cheap. She had got it cheap because it was built not of any reputable stone or even of brick, but of a local chalk going by the name of clunch: a soft stuff formerly in some esteem for internal decorative purposes in the dwellings of the rich, but now commonly employed for exterior and structural walls only in the hovels of the poor. It was more durable, however, than might have been supposed. What it seemingly couldn't do was to turn corners, and a fortuitous consequence of this was the patchy use of random supplies of brick or stone at every angle of the building to a surprisingly pleasing effect of the picturesque. Ruth had taken it because, with three disfathered children to think of, she had judged it important to have a dwelling roomy enough for at least the sporadic reception of numerous friends both old and young. It was an instance of her sagacity, but it hadn't made for any great ease in the way of domestic economy, particularly as the house stood in that sort of isolation which rustic purveyors of casual labour, male and female alike, were coming to regard as quite beyond the range of a pushbike. And in fact Ruth and her children now did entirely for themselves. Unless indeed one counted the pony, Smoky Joe, who was quite as hard working as any of them.

So much for Boxes (which Tim said ought to be called Clunches). When staying there Gilbert Averell was very aware of himself as of a sedentary habit. He knew that, if left there on his own, he couldn't cope with the place for a week. Yet he was fond of the country, and fond of country pursuits in a spectator's fashion. Had he long ago established a joint household with Ruth, as a bachelor brother might very reasonably do with a divorced sister clearly indisposed to second marriage, he would by now be settled in a way of life which at bottom would have suited him very well. What better situation could a private scholar have desired: a quiet domesticity within a couple of hours of the libraries in London, within an hour of the Bodleian in Oxford? The absurdity of his making this trip to England in a kind of disguise, and the embarrassingly improper motive underlying the fact, constituted a sort of symbolic representation of error not now to be repaired.

The car's approach had been heard from the house, and mother and daughters were waiting for him at the front door. Ruth was her unchanging self: bright-eyed and alert, but thinner than you felt she ought to be, in the manner sometimes to be observed in people who never allow themselves time to sit down. Kate and Gillian, on the other hand, had changed considerably. It wasn't just that their hair was differently done, as it might be from one day to the next. They were both taller and both more nubile – if that was the proper word. And they were these things, of course, in identical degree. He knew that the twins put in quite a lot of time differentiating themselves each from the other, but it was a struggle in which Nature gave them no assistance. And their uncle suspected that if they appeared not so identical in temperament as they did before a looking glass the difference was only achieved as more or less a put-up job. A single glance at them, incidentally, told him how imperfect as well as superficial was that resemblance of his own to his friend the Prince de Silistrie which had landed him in an undignified masquerade that he didn't yet know whether he was going to divulge to

Ruth or not.

That Kate and Gillian had been putting on their final inches since he last saw them was a reproach to him that he felt even as he scrambled from the car. It must be longer than he had been vaguely reckoning since he last visited Boxes.

'Gilbert, how splendid to see you!' Ruth said when she had kissed him and presided over her daughters accepting the same mode of greeting. She spoke with a lightness of air, just short of gaiety, which seemed to tell Averell one thing at once. If there was grave and urgent trouble about Tim it hadn't yet been communicated to, or discovered by, Tim's sisters. And the twins themselves made an immediate announcement that appeared to confirm this.

'And just in time,' Gillian said. 'We're off tomorrow.'

'To Rome,' Kate said. 'Just the two of us. Isn't that super? Not that we don't wish Mummy would come.'

'Quite impossible,' Ruth said, maintaining her carefree note. 'Smoky Joe would pine away. And the girls are quite old enough–'

'Mummy!' Kate and Gillian exclaimed simultaneously – one in ridicule and one in mock-indignation, but with an identical toss of the head.

'It sounds a bold plan for mere children,' Averell said – humorously, as would be expected of him. He turned aside briefly to pay off his driver. 'Are you going to put up in a pub?' he then asked.

'Well, no.' Kate made this admission with reluctance. 'Mummy has some friends in Rome. Almost relations, it seems, in a distant way. Gillian says everybody ought to have foreign relations, provided they *are* decently distant. I say we don't need any, because we have you, Uncle Gilbert. As a quasi-foreigner, one may say.'

Averell picked up his suitcase and followed the Barcrofts into the house. His nieces, he told himself, were at least still at a stage he remembered: that of constantly trying out an expanding vocabulary. But they must be at the beginning of almost the last of their school holidays. There would be a lot to talk about in the way of their future plans. But what about Tim? There was as yet no sign of him.

He went up to his room, and found with satisfaction that it was the one with its own bathroom. One had to be pretty elderly, at once to think about that. To the girls between themselves he was no doubt 'dear old Uncle Gilbert'. He washed and un-packed, getting out the three small presents he had brought along with him. They were minute expensive things of what he thought of as the cosmetic order, and had been chosen from a list with which he had been provided against such occasions by a Frenchwoman of considerable fashion. It seemed strange to be handing such objects to schoolgirls – rather like taking a box of cigars to a nephew still at Rugby or Marlborough. When he went downstairs again it was time for tea.

'But it isn't Rome,' Kate said at once, 'simply because eligible chaperonage is on tap there.' The girls were clearly so full of their coming adventure that they had no disposition to talk about anything else. 'There are two Romes, you see. Which means one for Gillian and one for me.'

'Two Romes? A respectable one and an underworld one, do you mean?' Averell was now urgently wanting to know about Tim, but felt he had to play.

'Well, it might be seen that way,' Gillian said. 'There's the Rome of Cicero and Pliny the Younger, and all those virtuous bores. And there's the Rome of the bad old Popes. Borgias and people like that.'

'I see. And have you tossed up?'

'Yes, we've tossed up. And I've got classical Rome and Kate's got the Renaissance.'

'I think you underestimate the complexity of the situation.' Averell accepted scones, butter, and Ruth's strawberry jam – justly judged incomparable. 'There are innumerable Romes, each packed tight upon the other. It's a regard in which Freud declared

56

Rome to resemble the human mind.'

This information was received with respect. Kate and Gillian, although their frivolous presents had been received with rapture, were no doubt young intellectuals in the making. Averell wondered how much of their brother's vision of society they received as gospel. If the girls also took up demonstrating and sitting-in in a big way it would come a little hard on Ruth, although Ruth would be entirely loyal to them. And Ruth, after all, was as committed as Tim to the theory of a disintegrating social order. (And who in his senses is not? It was darkly that Averell asked himself this question, in the hinterland of which lay his sense of himself as involved in an 'irrelevant' course of life.)

'We've had to get new passports,' Kate said suddenly. 'The photographs make us look like nothing on earth. But I suppose all passports do. You must show us yours, Uncle Gilbert.'

'So I must,' Averell said – with a nonchalance masking ludicrous alarm. And he added, very quickly, 'But what have you both put down under "profession"? Is it "Schoolgirl"? Whatever you put, you know, will follow you around for years.' He felt he had to labour this red herring. 'What about "Scholar-elect of Somerville College, Oxford"?'

'It would be a bold prolepsis,' Gillian said – blessedly falling to the vocabulary lure. 'We've just put "Student", as a matter of fact. It's noncommittal and far-reaching. You might use it yourself, Uncle Gilbert. What do you actually put?'

Averell couldn't remember what he did put – and was not in a position to refresh his memory in the matter.

'"Scholar",' he said at random (and improbably). And he added, almost at a gabble, 'T S Eliot once told me he put "Company Director". It got him a lot more respect, he said, than if he'd put "Poet".'

'Or "Author of *The Waste Land*",' Kate said. 'That would have puzzled them.'

The twins were both so pleased with this, and with an uncle who, in the dark ages, had owned so distinguished an acquaintance, that they fortunately forgot about passports, and began bringing their aged kinsman up to date on the present state of English poetry. They liked Philip Larkin – chiefly (Gillian said) because they both owned an antiquarian side, but also because he also reminded them of their Uncle Gilbert. But did he know Anthony Thwaite? Did he know Adrian Mitchell? Had he read *The Apeman Cometh?* Averell suffered this bombardment happily. And it didn't particularly disturb him that the girls hadn't so much as mentioned their brother. Tim was among those major facts of

58

life that can be taken for granted. And was famous. Everything that Tim was doing, everybody must already know.

Tea was over – including that cherry cake with a superabundance of cherries that it had been recalled Uncle Gilbert peculiarly approved of. Averell felt what a fool he had been not to see more of these girls. At the same time he was quite glad when they jumped simultaneously to their feet and departed on the various appointed tasks of the late afternoon. It was clear that, in the domestic way, they backed up their mother with all necessary vigour. Perhaps for the first time, it came vividly to Gilbert Averell that through long school terms, and for many years, Ruth and Smoky Joe had been coping with Boxes alone.

'Ruth,' Averell said, 'I'm wondering more and more about Tim. Tell me now.'

6

'It's rather vague,' Ruth Barcroft said. She spoke hesitantly, and a small rattle of china came from the tray on which she was stacking the tea things for removal. Both these phenomena surprised Averell. 'I don't even know,' she said, 'where Tim is.'

This remark too – or the tone of it – was puzzling. No doubt a mother likes to be kept informed about the movements of her children, but it had to be supposed that a twenty-two-year-old son might reasonably drop out of contact for brief periods now and then.

'He wouldn't tell me,' Ruth said.

This, if it accounted for the manner of Ruth's last speech, was perplexing in itself, and Averell waited for some further information. But Ruth was silent, her attention being apparently given up to the neat brushing of crumbs from one plate to another.

'Was this in a letter?' Averell asked cautiously.

'He rang up.' Ruth made yet another pause. 'Gilbert, do they let you ring up from – from police-stations, and places like that?'

'Good heavens, Ruth! But, yes. At least I

expect that in some cases they do. Are you afraid Tim has been arrested again?'

'It might be that, mightn't it? Or he may even be in gaol by now. The telephone call came just before I rang you up in Paris.'

'I see. But he made no secret of that last affair, did he? I seem to remember your hearing about it at once, and his coming home to Boxes as soon as they bailed him out.'

'Yes, and it was even rather funny. Tim had to go and report himself to Constable Capper in the village, and it embarrassed Capper frightfully. But this may be different.'

'It may be altogether different, Ruth, and have nothing to do with the police at all.' Averell was astonished by the extent to which his sister appeared to be upset by Tim's disappearance, which was still for no longer than the inside of a week. 'Let's face it, my dear. The boy may have all sorts of reasons for being a bit coy about his whereabouts for a time. For instance, there may be a girl in the case.'

'He'd tell me, wouldn't he, if there was a girl?'

'In some circumstances he might.' Averell was astonished this time by such a flight of maternal innocence. 'But he'd be no more likely to tell you than to tell his sisters if he were having a shot – perhaps even a first shot – at something strictly dishonourable. Having a quiet weekend, say, with his vice-

chancellor's well-preserved siren of a wife.'
Averell checked himself, aware of having a
very uncertain touch at this sort of thing,
and doubting whether it was appropriate in
face of his sister's evident forebodings. 'No
point,' he ended briefly, 'in ducking such
perfectly normal things.'

'It didn't sound like that.'

'Well, Ruth, you haven't told me how it *did*
sound.'

'Like something I didn't like. I'm glad I'm
getting the girls away.'

'In heaven's name, my dear! You haven't
arranged this trip for them because of how
Tim sounded on a telephone?'

'Of course not. Rome was all arranged
months ago. It's just fortunate it's now, if
something really bad is turning up. Don't
you still smoke that pipe, Gilbert? You know
I don't mind it.'

'You still haven't alarmed me, Ruth, I'm
thankful to say.' (This wasn't quite true.)
'But perhaps you'd better tell me *all* that
Tim said when he rang up. In the first place,
why did he ring up when he did?'

'Because he'd arranged to come straight
home at the end of term, and now he wasn't
going to.'

'So he was probably ringing up from
Oxford?'

'I don't think so. He seems to have been a
good deal out of Oxford lately. Under-

graduates come and go as they please much more than they used to do. Particularly in a final year, when they mayn't be in college more than a couple of times in a week.'

'I suppose it's reasonable enough. They're grown up, after all. But it wasn't like that when I was at Cambridge. Managing un-detected French leave was part of the fun.'

'I'm not sure that Tim goes in for fun, Gilbert. In spite of your jokes about vice-chancellors' wives.'

'In fact, it would be student politics – and of the activist sort, as they say – that would take him here and there?'

'Well, yes – and what would be called student journalism too, I suppose. Have you heard of *En Vedette?* It's a paper he works for. I don't even know what it means.'

'You print a thing *en vedette* if you set it up in very large type. But a *vedette* is also a guard or sentinel. So I suppose there's meant to be a double meaning.'

'I see.' Ruth was always impressed by her brother's knowledge of the French tongue. 'Well, Tim writes articles for it. And he goes to those stupid demonstrations and sit-downs, if that's what they're called, and takes photographs at them. He likes to snap policemen grabbing banners, and shoving around on horseback, and all that sort of thing. Of course, it's just high spirits, but I feel it might always lead to trouble. And Tim seems to me too serious for the nonsense side of student activities. To my mind, he usually shows very good judgement about the issues he feels to be important.'

'I'd not doubt that for a moment.' Ruth's firm defence of her son was thought by Averell to be very much in order. 'But please go back to the telephone call. What more did he say?'

'At first he just said that he happened to be pretty busy at present, so he wouldn't be coming home during this vacation after all. I was very disappointed, as you can imagine, but of course I tried not to show it. But, somehow, I was alarmed as well.'

'Why should you be alarmed, Ruth?'

'It was something I felt about Tim's state of mind, rather than about what he had said. So I did press him a little – as I oughtn't to have done. I said how nice it would be if he could at least see something of his sisters before they went to Rome. It was silly.'

'Well, yes. It was rather.' Averell, although he didn't see his sister all that often, had managed to preserve with her this sort of immediate frankness in speech. 'It wasn't as if the girls were going away for months and months. Tim might well have been a little annoyed.'

'I don't think he was, Gilbert. But he did seem agitated.'

'*Agitated?*' This wasn't at all Averell's notion of his nephew.

'He blurted out that if the girls were at home it was all the more reason for his not turning up.'

'How very odd! Do you think something may have overtaken him which he feels would make him distressingly poor company? One of those sudden undergraduate depressions, for instance, or an irrational phobia?'

'He did say something more, and it doesn't fit in with anything of that sort. He said that if he did come home he would probably be bringing unwelcome attentions in his wake. Can you make anything of that, Gilbert?'

'I don't know that I can. But wait! Perhaps Tim has got mixed up in some student affair that's going to make a lot of news when it breaks. That might mean journalists and photographers prowling round Boxes on the hunt for him – and for the rest of you as well. Tim certainly wouldn't like that at all.'

'I hadn't thought of that.' It was an index of the depth of Ruth's anxiety that she seemed to embrace this rather remote possibility as a cheerful reading of the matter. 'It would be quite something,' she added with a momentary attempt at gaiety, 'to have even one mysterious stranger prowling around Boxes with a camera or a notebook.

We sometimes don't see anybody for a week on end.'

During this conference, brother and sister had been sitting on either side of the drawing-room fireplace: Ruth with her tea equipage still beside her, and Averell with his back to a tall French window a good deal obscured by a holly bush under imperfect control. And as Ruth uttered her last words her eyes suddenly rounded, and her gaze fixed itself over her brother's shoulder.

'And there *is* somebody!' she cried.

Averell's was a high-backed chair, and as a consequence of this he had to jump to his feet and swing round before he could gain a notion of what Ruth was talking about. He achieved these movements, however, with a celerity that must have surprised him had he paused to think about it. But this he was far from doing, and he was halfway to the window before a holly branch swung across it – thereby obscuring the face, and even the presence, of somebody who had been peering into the room. And now there came a clatter from outside, as if a flowerpot or watering can had been kicked over, followed by the sound of rapidly running footsteps. Averell pulled open the French window in time to see an unidentifiable male figure vanish round a corner of the house.

Averell, extremely angry, had no other thought than of hot pursuit. It was intolerable that his sister should thus be spied upon, even if nothing particularly sinister were involved. And it didn't occur to him, despite the curious context in which this impertinence had taken place, that anything of the kind was so. His reading had persuaded him that peeping and eavesdropping (often achieved *en plein air* by an adroit exploitation of hedges and ditches) were staple employments among the humbler sections of rural society. And for some reason he was quite confident, as he himself rounded an angle of the building, that he was going to catch the offender. When he did so, and if the intruder proved to be of mature years, he could probably do no more than utter threatening words about trespass and the police. If a juvenile was concerned he could be told he was to be led off to his father for a good hiding. Not that Averell would in fact do anything of the kind, so all that he was achieving was vindicating to himself a certain capacity for action. And unfortunately it proved entirely unrewarding. The miscreant had vanished, and the first person Averell encountered was Gillian, returning from some evening chore among the poultry.

'Good heavens!' Gillian said. 'Why ever so hot and bothered?'

'Nothing in the least important.' Averell had rather resented this description of himself, although it was fair enough. 'Only some confounded yokel peering outrageously through the window at your mother and myself.'

'Oh, come, Uncle Gilbert! He must just have been looking for the back door or something. We don't go in for inquisitive yokels round about Boxes. They're all too utterly absorbed in their own minuscule affairs.' Gillian was clearly rather pleased with her command of this phrase. 'And nobody,' she added as an afterthought, 'would hope for a glimpse of incestuous orgy through our drawing-room window.'

'I suppose not.' Averell turned back with his niece towards the house, chiefly concerned to conceal that he was a little shocked by this freedom of fancy on the part of a schoolgirl. But he was also wondering whether the episode just concluded had prevented Ruth from giving him any further useful information about that telephone call, or whether he now knew as much about the occasion of Tim's staying away from Boxes as she did. And what would Tim mean by a phrase like 'unwelcome attentions'? It might after all be something in the area that Averell himself had rather frivolously suggested: 'girl trouble', as the young people now succinctly expressed it. Tim might have tangled with a nymphomaniac female who would pursue him to his mother's house and scandalously clamour at its gates. But this wasn't really plausible, and it was foolish to imagine that whenever somebody of Tim's age got into trouble it was a matter of sex rearing its ugly head. What might be called a political reading of the mystery was much more likely to be on the mark, and what Tim had in mind was the hazard of his family's being upset by the arrival of a policeman or some officer of a court bearing a summons or a warrant or similar engine of the law.

And this view of the matter assumed a higher probability later that evening. It seemed that it was Ruth's turn to cook the dinner, and to her daughters, therefore, fell the duty of entertaining their uncle at a pre-prandial hour. With some solemnity they made him go down to the cellar and choose a bottle of wine. Kate uncorked it with enormous care, and with an equal precision Gillian set it down at what he pointed to as the appropriate distance from the drawing-room fire. Then the girls sat down and prepared to chatter. Or, rather, he thought it was going to be like that but it turned out slightly differently.

'Uncle Gilbert,' Kate asked sharply, 'has my mother talked to you about Tim?'

For Kate to say 'my mother' like that was very formal; it might almost be said to be out of Jane Austen. So Averell felt that something serious was being heralded. And as the question was calculated to force his confidence, and as Kate would normally be punctilious in such a regard, he was constrained to feel that his nieces had their anxieties too.

'Why, yes,' he said. 'She's disappointed he isn't coming home.'

'She says,' Gillian said, 'that it's nothing, and that Tim's just very busy because of his exams at the end of next term. But of course he can be as busy as he likes that way here.'

'And have us waiting on him hand and foot,' Kate said.

'Particularly foot,' Gillian said. 'We run and fetch him his slippers.'

'But hand as well. The brimming glass thrust into it.'

'As a special privilege we're allowed to stuff his pipe for him or watch him shave.'

'And a handkerchief soaked in eau-de-Cologne is applied to the wearied brow.'

'If you have something to say,' Averell said, 'don't shy away from it.'

'We're sorry,' Gillian said more soberly. 'I suppose we're rather nervous, as a matter of fact. We're a family almost disgustingly without secrets, as a rule. But now Mummy doesn't know we suspect anything's wrong, and we do. So it's awkward.'

'Just what do you suspect is wrong?'

'It's not exactly that, really,' Kate said. 'It's just that we have a piece of specific inform-ation. We noticed it in a newspaper, and

Mummy didn't, and somehow we didn't want to call her attention to it.'

'In case it was all nonsense, or irrelevant,' Gillian said. 'It was a paragraph saying that two young men whom we know are Tim's very close friends have hit a bad patch. Something about a judge having issued an injunction, whatever that is, and their having ignored it, and so its being a contempt.'

'*Whatever* that is,' Kate said. 'But it sounds pretty pompous and portentous.'

'And you think Tim may be standing by to help, or something like that?' Averell paused to consider his own question. 'I can't see that he wouldn't simply let your mother know about that. It can't be so very terrible. Less alarming, really, than vague conjecture.'

'It was a great shock to my mother,' Kate said, resuming her more severe manner, 'when they locked Tim up. She tried to conceal it, but it was. And I've no doubt she's imagining the same thing now.'

'Yes,' Averell said quietly. 'As a matter of fact, she is.'

'And Tim's a very tiresome young man. Tiresome Tim is how he was born, I think.' Gillian produced these unfavourable judgements vehemently but not to an effect of any great conviction. 'Oh, dear! I forgot the sherry.'

The sherry was produced, and Ruth made a brief appearance to share it. She then returned to the kitchen; Kate went to the dining-room to lay the table; Gillian disappeared in order to ensure the nocturnal comfort of Smoky Joe. So there was no further talk about what was so plainly in everybody's head. There was, in fact, none until, shortly before bedtime, Tim Barcroft made his unexpected homecoming to Boxes.

7

The young man had let himself in with a latchkey – and surely very quietly, since nobody had heard a sound until he was in the room. Perhaps he had intended a childish effect of surprise. And surprise of a sort he did achieve: this by striding straight to the window, drawing back a curtain, and peering intently into the dark. It was the window, as it happened, through which the mysterious intruder had done his peeping a few hours before.

Averell decided that he didn't at all like this theatrical behaviour. It was disturbing Ruth, and his nieces were clearly uncertain whether or not they were being entertained to an obscure joke. Yet in a moment it was over, and Tim, seemingly much at his ease, was standing in front of the fireplace and glancing at his relations smilingly.

'Here's the prodigal son come home,' he said. 'And the fatted calf actually all ready prepared! Uncle Gilbert's the fatted calf. Let's fall to and devour him.'

'Tim, dear,' Ruth said.

'Yes, it's me.' Tim bent down swiftly and kissed his mother, and when he straightened up again his manner had changed. 'Did I worry you on the telephone?' he asked. 'It was stupid of me, and I'm sorry. There's absolutely nothing to worry about. I was upset by something so trivial that it would be idiotic to talk about it. Short of the fatted calf, is there anything in the larder? I'm splendidly hungry.'

Much as if they really were in the habit of scurrying to fetch their brother his slippers, Kate and Gillian vanished into the kitchen. And their mother, too, rose.

'I must take a look at your bedroom, dear,' she said. And she walked rather slowly from the room. It was an action that gave Averell an immediate pause. The girls had been thinking only of feeding their brother on demand. But Ruth's thus immediately with-drawing had been prompted by something else, and its effect on her brother was that of having had a ball swiftly lobbed into his court. Ruth had decided that, despite Tim's so briskly asserting there was nothing to worry about, something was on foot that men had best get down to together. And now it looked as if she was right.

'I'm damned glad you're here,' Tim said abruptly. 'I'd no idea. But I'll have this quick meal by the fire, talking any nonsense I can. Please play it that way, Uncle Gilbert. And then we'll get them off to bed.'

'Very well.' For the moment, Averell could

think of nothing more to say. He was wondering whether Tim had gone off his head, and a glance at the young man was far from reassuring. It was as if, alone with his uncle, he had fleetingly let fall a mask. 'Wild eyed' would be the right description of him – that, and possibly 'haggard' as well. But perhaps it was simply that he was, for some reason, physically exhausted. He looked as if he had been travelling fast and far, and very uncomfortably as well.

The three women returned, and Tim sat down to his meal. He drank a glass of the remaining wine, but didn't finish the bottle. He made no offer to explain himself further, but talked casually of various Oxford or family occasions. Averell sensed that he was putting into this a considerable effort of the will, and he did his best to back the boy up. Kate and Gillian were perplexed, but their feelings seemed to stop short of dismay. Ruth signalled her composure by a steady application to something she was knitting. Were they accustomed to Tim's putting on odd turns? Averell had never heard of anything of the sort. Nor could he remember on any previous visit to Boxes an atmosphere of repressed discomfort possessing the entire household for an hour on end. Did it arise now from a sense that Tim was only half-attending to his own talk; that he was, in fact, listening for something else? One of the charms of Boxes lay in its secluded situation; it hadn't a window from which another dwelling could be seen; the spire of a distant village church was the only evidence that man had ever set stone upon stone in England. Ruth, when in rare moments of depression she thought about selling up, would declare that such privacy was what people were now prepared to pay any money for. Averell was suddenly conscious that there was another side to this medal. Only imagine any sort of lawlessness around and that degree of isolation assumed a disadvantageous aspect. The night was very silent now; there was nothing to be heard except the ripple of the stream that ran through the garden; the proverbial crack of a twig that signals danger in juvenile romances would certainly sound like a pistol shot.

'I want to talk to Uncle Gilbert about something entirely boring. But it will keep until you people go to bed.'

Tim had come out with this announcement as if it was the politest thing in the world, but it brought the family evening to a close on a further note of constraint, all the same. Ruth and her daughters departed, leaving Averell so surprised that for some moments he said nothing at all.

'Wasn't that on the cavalier side?' he then asked mildly.

'Bloody rude, I suppose. But it can't be

helped – and there's more to come, I'm afraid. Uncle Gilbert, has anything out of the way happened at Boxes since you came?'

'Good lord, no! And I only arrived this afternoon.' Averell hesitated for a moment, and reflected that the mode of Tim's own arrival lent a certain conceivable relevance to one very trivial episode. 'There was somebody snooping around outside the house at teatime, as a matter of fact. Would you call that out of the way?'

For a moment Tim made no reply, but his uncle could see him stiffen in his chair. Then he sprang out of it and left the room, to return a minute later carrying a shotgun and a box of cartridges.

'Comforting,' he said. 'I thought of it more than once on the way down.'

Standing in front of the fireplace, and beneath the astonished eyes of his kinsman, Tim loaded both barrels of the weapon.

'It's not often that I manage to pot so much as a rabbit,' he said. 'But the thing could deal out a fairly good peppering, all the same. There'd be a howl or two, wouldn't you say?'

Averell didn't say. He was wondering whether this exhibition merely astonished him, which would be reasonable, or whether it frightened him as well. For the moment, at least, he gave himself the benefit of the doubt. And now he found that he was alone in his sister's drawing-room, with leisure to indulge in any further speculations he chose. Tim, with his gun under his arm much as if he were prowling one of the paddocks surrounding the property, had gone into the hall and shot the bolts on the front door; seconds later he was moving from room to room on the ground floor, closing windows and securing shutters. If the afternoon's snooper returned he would now certainly be thwarted in his snooping, or even in a tolerably determined attempt to break in. Averell, as if infected by whatever imaginings his nephew was prompted by, fell to reviewing in his mind's eye the entire layout of Boxes. It was scarcely well-calculated, he decided, to repel organized assault. But that, surely, was something altogether too extravagant to conceive.

Tim returned to the drawing-room, and quietly laid the gun down beside his chair.

'Uncle,' he said, 'would you say you had a certain authority with my mother and sisters?'

'I don't know. I've certainly never done all that to earn anything of the kind, Tim. But, yes – perhaps.'

'They must be got away.'

'Got away!'

'All of them, I mean. Mummy must go with the girls to Rome tomorrow. We can bring it off, if we're firm. I'll be staying to look after the livestock. And they all three simply adore last-moment plans.'

'There would be room on any flight at this time of year, I suppose.' Averell, not unnaturally, was astounded by all this, but found Tim's earnestness and vehemence persuasive. 'Only we'd have to be pretty brisk at putting it across at the breakfast table.'

'We'll manage it. We must. I'm telling you.'

'Tim, I don't know what to make of you. Begin at the beginning, for heaven's sake! Just what is this all about?'

'I don't know.'

'But that simply doesn't make sense.'

'I simply don't know. But there it is – what's been happening.'

'*Precisely* what–?'

'I decided not to come home, you see, because I felt they might follow me. I'd lie low somewhere else until I got the hang of it. But then I had this other thought.'

'Just what other thought?' There must have been complete bewilderment in Averell's voice. Tim wasn't given to speaking in riddles.

'They'd know where my home was – or they'd find out. So they might come to Boxes anyway. And it sounds as if they had.'

'Tim, who on earth are "they"?' Deranged persons, Averell believed, frequently got round to talking about a 'them' who were essentially figments of the imagination. Had

Tim turned into such a one? Averell discovered with relief that he thought not. But from this it followed that the boy had actually got into deep water of some sort. And it could scarcely be with the police, or with the law in any form. You don't, if you're sane – and Tim, he reiterated to himself, *was* sane – load a shotgun in any such exigency as that. But at least there was something to explore here.

'Tim,' he said, 'you talk as if some gang of criminals was after you. If that's so, why don't you go to the police?'

'*I* can't do that. You know I can't.'

'What nonsense! Anybody can go to the police.' As he said this robustly, Averell was just conscious of the fact – and it was a mere oddity – that at this moment he himself might find contact with the police something he'd avoid if he could. Not, of course, in a situation of any real gravity. But if he did so contact them, there was a probability that, sooner or later, he'd have an awkward misdemeanour – or was it a felony? – to explain.

'The fuzz aren't my friends exactly,' Tim elaborated with an air of patience. 'They sat me down and they stood round me. I wasn't clobbered, or anything like that. But it wasn't nice.'

'It certainly can't have been.' Averell was perfectly willing to acknowledge to himself

that here was territory legitimately trau-
matic, so to speak, in the experience even of
an entirely level-headed young man.

'But it isn't just that, Uncle Gilbert. It's all
so confused, and I have to try to think it out.
As I said, at the moment I simply haven't a
clue. But, first, there's this urgent thing.
They might do a kidnap, mightn't they?
Here at Boxes. And then I'd be helpless. I'd
have to do anything they asked.' Tim paused.
'For it *would* be like that, wouldn't it?'

'I suppose it might.' Averell saw that the
proposition he was acquiescing in was
comprehensible in itself but surrounded by
total mystery. He also saw that Tim was
unaware of the fragmentary and inconse-
quent nature of such information as he was
giving, and that this was probably the
consequence of extreme fatigue. 'When did
you last get some sleep?' he asked.

'Sleep?' The word was repeated by Tim as
if it was something he'd just heard of but
couldn't very certainly identify. 'Oh, quite
some time ago, it must have been.'

'Then hadn't we better go to bed now, and
tackle this in the morning?'

'This?'

'Look, Tim. I always wake up quite early.
I'll make some tea and bring it to you, so
that we can get things sorted out before the
household's up and around – or your new
plan has to be mooted.'

'It's an idea.' Tim moved uncertainly on his chair. He seemed quite to have lost the power of action which had taken him round the house, locking it up; and he had lost, too, the incisiveness with which he had ordered his womenfolk about. He didn't even seem to be remembering his gun. 'There was a boy at school who said he always did his maths when asleep. The answer was ready to write down when he woke up. The working, too, I suppose. They always insisted on the working. I can't think why, provided the answer was correct.' Tim produced an enormous and quite healthy-seeming yawn. 'Perhaps it will come to me in a dream. Just how it started, I mean. Or *why* it started. Do you think?'

'It's worth a try. And, by the way, I'm a very light sleeper myself, Tim. So if there was the slightest disturbance round the place I'd be aware of it, and rouse you at once.'

'Super, Uncle Gilbert.' Surprisingly and rather touchingly, Tim got meekly to his feet. 'Is there anything I can get you first?' Tim glanced at Averell in a kind of sleepy appraisal, and was possibly made aware of his advancing years. 'A hot water bottle, perhaps?'

'No thank you, my dear Tim. I'll be fine.'

So they went upstairs to bed. And it was Averell who took charge of the gun. He had renewed doubts about Tim's entire sanity.

And this made him feel there was something to be said for the fantastic and arbitrary plan of packing Ruth off with her daughters on the following morning. If Tim could manage the livestock, he could manage Tim – or so he believed – until any brain-storm was over. And if there was no brain-storm but, on the contrary, some real if still wholly mysterious threat – then with luck the two of them might manage that together.

8

On these occasions – rare in recent years – when Averell spent a night at Boxes it was his habit to take a turn in the garden before going to bed. Tonight Tim's persuasion that danger lurked there had to be deferred to, even if it was hard quite to believe in it. But at least it was possible to take a glance through the bedroom window, and Averell treated himself to this as soon as he had got into his pyjamas. He pulled back the curtain, and made to raise the sash thus exposed. It proved to come up no more than some four inches, and was then held by a catch which it took him a few moments to locate. He now recalled that all the windows were equipped in this way, and he even had a dim memory that this had been done on his own advice. The house being regularly occupied only by the three women, and quite often by Ruth alone, it had seemed an obvious measure of prudence. And it must have been these catches, among other things, that Tim had been checking on the ground floor.

The garden was bathed in moonlight, and when Averell switched off the electric lamps he had previously turned on this milder illumination tumbled into the room in a pleasing way. He threw up the sash when he had released it, stuck his head out, and told himself that, for April, it was an uncommonly mild night. Far away, the line of the downs stood out against a clear sky in gentle undulations the traversing of which he would normally be looking forward to as a principal employment while at Boxes. In the garden itself he could readily identify one familiar object and another, even down to the big garden roller that never seemed to get itself shifted out of the little hollow into which it sank perceptibly year by year. Level lawns made no part of Ruth's programme for survival. What was probably not surviving was the group of elms beyond the stream, since in this part of the country he knew the ravages of Dutch Elm Disease to have been pervasive. But as the trees were not yet in leaf he couldn't be certain of this in the moonlight, and he resolved to go and inspect them, and much else, after breakfast. It was a moment before he recalled that this was an inapposite proposal in the context of his present untoward situation. Yet the garden itself was at least reassuringly peaceful, and he lingered at his window for some time before lowering the sash again to the position in which it was possible to secure it while still admitting fresh air (which was something it would never have occurred to him to solicit *sous les toits de Paris*). He then left the curtain drawn back and went to bed (again in his more or less adoptive language, *au clair de lune*).

Bright moonlight, like nightingales or cicadas, can be a nuisance when one wants to go to sleep. Or frogs, for that matter. Averell was just learnedly remembering the perplexing fact that the ancient Greeks and Romans held all these pests in high regard when sleep abruptly overtook him. It had been, after all, a taxing day.

Tim (as if he were an ancient Greek or Roman himself) had been hoping for a dream of a mysteriously enlightening order. But it was to Averell himself that such a dream came – although its enlightenment, indeed, was to be of a delayed action sort. It wasn't an edifying dream; on the contrary, it was grossly and violently sexual in a fashion wholly perplexing if one were to consider how remote from anything of the kind had been all his recent preoccupations. Yet some of these undoubtedly made themselves felt in what his slumbering mind cooked up. For one thing, the ego of the dream was by no means very clearly Gilbert Averell. Indeed, people were choosing to believe that he was really King Charles II, that merry monarch who scattered his Maker's image through the land, and he seemed not to be doing much to disillusion them. The activities of this conceivably composite figure (which it would be by no means proper to set down upon the page) kept on being vexatiously interrupted by a little man from Hull, who went by the improbable name of Stendhal. Stendhal was an outrageous *voyeur*, and he kept bobbing up at the most inconvenient times. Fortunately Stendhal disliked music, being very much one to delight in treasons, stratagems and spoils. Contrive as a background to those desperate embraces a sufficiently shattering musical accompaniment, preferably Wagnerian, and Stendhal simply ceased to goggle and peer and faded away. And such an occasion made the climax of the dream. The Averell/Charles figure was striving after some positively acrobatic achievement amid a tumble of crashing chords; there was a final great clash of cymbals; Averell woke up.

It must be admitted again that all this held little of edification; and neither was it particularly remarkable in itself. What was of some psychological interest was the fact that Averell's moment of awakening was attended by a notable confusion of the senses, or mess-up in what the erudite call the coenaesthesia. The loud bang hadn't been a loud bang at all; it had been a brilliant and momentary flash of light.

Averell's first coherent thought was to wait

for the thunder clap. He even began counting, which is supposed to be the way to tell how far off such an electrical discharge has taken place. But there was no thunder. There had just been the flash of lightning and nothing else at all.

He continued to listen, and suddenly heard the sound of what might have been something falling over in the garden. His dream had scarcely been such as to restore the energies wrested from him by the fatigues of the preceding day. Nevertheless he sprang out of bed, hastened to the window, groped for the catch, flung up the sash, thrust out his head. There was nothing out of the way to be seen. Had there been, he'd still not have seen it – the moon having dipped over the horizon and departed.

But now Gilbert Averell was entirely collected, and very well able to decide that his dream – or at least his awakening from it – had been controlled by some actual event in the external world. And he could do one of two things: either stick his head under the bedclothes and endeavour to go to sleep again, or proceed to investigate forthwith. Finding that he was decidedly for the latter course, he switched on the bedroom light. The first object his eye fell upon was Tim Barcroft's shotgun. It had quite a reassuring look.

But, of course, he wouldn't have a notion

of how to fire the thing. Were he to attempt to do so, no pepperings, no howlings would result. Realizing this – and realizing, too, that whatever had happened afforded some colour to the disturbing notions in Tim's head – Averell picked up the gun, opened his door, and went quietly along the corridor to Tim's room. The moment had come when he and his nephew must tackle something together.

'Oh, bother!' Tim said, when given a good shake. 'I was having a marvellous dream.' He sat up in bed. 'What's the matter, Uncle Gilbert? Are you ill?'

'Be quiet, Tim.' Averell found that he was whispering. 'And listen.' And he gave an account of his disconcerting experience. Tim listened intently, scrambling into his dressing gown and a pair of shoes the while.

'We'll take a look,' Tim said decidedly. 'Go on the offensive. It's the only thing.'

'Very well.'

'And give me that gun, for goodness sake. You look like a Yeoman of the Guard with his halberd or something. There are a couple of electric torches in the hall.'

They crept downstairs, leaving Ruth and her daughters apparently undisturbed. Each armed with a torch, they went out through the front door, which Tim locked behind him. There was a clear sky, with all the proper constellations available for study had they been disposed to it. Nevertheless it was extremely dark, and Averell rapidly developed a sense that their foray could only be of a random and unconsidered sort. If there was no intruder around any longer, there was nothing to be done – except, of course, ring up the police and report the matter, which Tim was unwilling to do. But, if, on the other hand, Tim's belief in the probability of some violent attack had any basis at all, mucking around with torches in the dark was simply to create sitting (or almost sitting) targets in the most foolhardy manner. Messrs Barcroft and Averell, in fact, would have to improve their technique considerably if they were to keep their end up against mysterious adversaries while going it alone.

They turned a corner of the house, much as Averell had done during his earlier adventure that afternoon. And at once drama confronted them.

Drama confronted them in the light of Tim's torch, which was shining full upon a man out of a newspaper. It was thus that Averell instantly and not very accurately conceived the matter, since it is rather in TV playlets that one is being glared at through a stocking or similar filmy integument. The man now doing this ought perhaps to have been pointing a revolver or brandishing a bludgeon. Oddly enough, his immediate impulse upon being thus suddenly bathed in

90

light appeared to be defensive or evasive. He took a blundering sideways step which landed him rather heavily against the wall of the house. Something painful must have resulted, since he gave a yelp of mingled agony, indignation, and alarm. He then dodged first to one side and then to the other, much in the manner of a three-quarter proposing to evade a couple of lumbering forwards bearing down on him. Tim dropped his torch, stepped back, and unslung his shotgun. Averell found himself disliking this action very much, since he knew that the intruder, be his intentions ever so nefarious, ought not to be despatched out of hand. Averell, the beam of his own torch waving wildly in air, even tried to push the weapon away. A moment of deepened confusion resulted, and of this the ruffian took instant advantage. Turning tough, he punched Averell on the nose. Averell, who had not been entertained in any such fashion since leaving his private school, was much surprised and cried out in an undignified manner; he was also, for the moment, blinded by a watery suffusion of the eyes accompanied as by an effect of suddenly ignited fireworks. The ruffian then got in a sufficiently well-directed hack at Tim's shins to send him sprawling. And then he just disappeared. By the time the discomfited investigators had recovered themselves and their torches there was simply no chance of catching up with him.

They made a sober return to the front door. But, just before reaching it, Tim stopped and pointed upwards.

'There's your window, Uncle Gilbert,' he said. 'There's still a light in it. But no other lights. So they haven't woken up.'

'Which is at least something,' Averell said. His nose was still hurting a good deal. 'And I've come round to your view, Tim. We'd better get them all away.'

'And look! That's what he used to get up to your window.' Tim's torch had circled, and revealed a ladder that lay slanted on the lawn. 'You heard it tumble, didn't you? He pulled it down after him when he heard you coming at the window. He probably felt you might shin down it behind him.'

'I'd only have got it on the nose a few minutes earlier if I had, I suppose? Averell felt that this was a sadly feeble philosophical reflection. 'Why should he want to climb up to my window, anyway?' he asked. 'There's no sense in it.'

'Because he thought it was my window, of course.' Tim spoke impatiently and as if asserting something self-evident. 'The flash you saw was the chap turning on a torch and scanning the room through that chink at the bottom. You'd left it open, hadn't you? When he saw he'd got the wrong man he began to retreat. And that was when you jumped out of bed and made after him. Or in a fashion, you did.'

'In a fashion, yes.' Averell knew that he was unconvinced by this interpretation of the affair, but didn't quite know why. 'That wasn't quite the effect,' he said. 'Of the turning on of a torch, I mean. Of course I'd woken up on the instant. But it was much more like lightning. As I told you.'

For a moment Tim made no reply. He might even not have been listening. Then he pointed again at the ladder.

'I'd better tell you,' he said quietly. 'Two attempts on my life. And now this.'

They went back into the house. Tim locked the door and shot a couple of heavy bolts.

'Go to bed again, Uncle Gilbert,' he said with authority. 'I'll keep watch. And in the morning we'll do as we said. And we'll get the bastards – by God, we will!'

Averell heard a faint click – and was now so unnerved that he jumped at the sound.

'Always think of the safety-catch,' Tim said with a certain air of humour, 'before you walk upstairs with a gun. That's in the book of rules.'

9

It might well be true that Ruth Barcroft, like her daughters, adored last-moment plans. But there was nothing feather-headed about her, and her brother thought poorly of the chances of getting her abruptly out of Boxes and off to Rome. This would be particularly so if it had to be represented to her that the idea sprang from the notion of removing her from some obscure danger which her son and his uncle would be remaining to confront. Any such project was a non-starter of the most obvious sort.

On the other hand – Averell thought as he lay sleepless in bed – any other way of going about the thing would be disingenuous. He revolted strongly against anything of the kind – perhaps for the not very logical (but psychologically comprehensible) reason that he was himself involved in a petty deception which he now acknowledged to be of the most humiliating order. Certainly he didn't look forward a bit to the family's breakfast table conversation. He couldn't criticize Tim for urging him to bring to bear what Tim had called his 'authority' as titular head of the family, since the boy believed himself to

94

be facing a situation so grim that he must seize any weapon he could. But he didn't at all know how decently to back him up.

But when morning came the thing went pat. Tim said no more than, 'Why don't you go too, Mrs B? I'd adore running Boxes for a fortnight all on my own – and running Uncle Gilbert too.' And before his mother could reply, both Kate and Gillian were urging the plan like mad. It wasn't, Averell could see, that Tim had been confiding in them at daybreak, or even propounding the idea while giving no particular reasons at all. It was simply that the twins had been feeling it mean to leave their mother behind, and had apparently been saying so already; this and the fact that Ruth's friend in Rome had been imploring her to join the party. In face of all this Ruth allowed herself to be swept agreeably off her feet. In no time Tim was masterfully on the telephone to the airline, booking her flight and arranging that she should pick up traveller's cheques at her bank's branch at Heathrow, and making sundry other practical arrangements of the most irrevocable sort. By ten o'clock mother and daughters had disappeared in a hired car down the drive.

'And now,' Tim said briskly, 'we're off ourselves. It's just a matter of finding somebody to look after all that damned livestock, beginning with the confounded pony and ending with the bird-table for the finches and all that rubbish they keep hanging up for the tits.'

'Is this going to be quite fair?' Averell asked feebly. 'We didn't give them a hint we weren't going to stay put.' He was quite upset by this rapid revelation of his nephew's masculine disregard for some of the cherished interests of his womenfolk.

'To hell with all gentlemanlike feeling,' Tim said brutally. His spirits were rising in an irresistible way. 'I never believed that all's fair in love, but it damned well is in war. Old Totterdel will do. He's quite half-witted, of course, but he won't muck up those simple chores. And if he does manage to throttle Smoky Joe, so much the better. Those kids ought to be through with pony madness by now. It ceases to be decent when a girl ought to be turning her thoughts in the direction of eligible bipeds. And if Kate and Gillian weren't my sisters I'd be having a go at them by this time myself.'

'My dear Tim—'

'Okay, okay, Uncle Gilbert. I'm a bit off-balance, no doubt. And if I don't adore the brute creation, I admit I ought to. Think of that cat.'

'What cat?'

'Hat.'

'*Hat?*'

'Well, this cat was called Hat. Somebody's

96

joke, I suppose.' Tim looked round the empty garden of Boxes with a wariness now habitual with him. 'I owe my life to Hat. Come inside and I'll tell you.'

They went into the drawing-room, which seemed instantly to have taken on an untenanted look. Tim threw himself into a chair and began to speak with the air of a man intent upon lucid narrative.

'For some time, you see, I've been sharing some rooms in London with some other people. A *pied à terre*, as they used to say.'

'Just other young men?'

'No, not just other young men. A kind of commune thing, in a small way. You know what I mean.'

Averell didn't know that he did know. He was a poor authority, he told himself, on the ways of the more or less alienated young.

'Well?' he said.

'I happened to be all alone there – just for a couple of days. Except for this Hat. On the second morning the postman delivered a small parcel for me, and I was a bit surprised. The place wasn't a secret hideout, or anything of the kind, but I didn't reckon to get any mail there. It looked as if somebody had sent me a book. People are always sending people books that they think they ought to read. I took it into the living-room and put in on a table in the window. Hat was on the table too – and glowering at me in a hostile way he had with him. Fair enough. I don't much dig cats. But it occurred to me the brute was hungry, so I went into the little kitchen and opened a tin of some nasty stuff cats are supposed to eat. Hat must have got the smell of it at once, because I was just back in the doorway when he jumped off the table and knocked this parcel to the floor. It's not a thing cats often do, so perhaps he was really very hungry indeed. Anyway, that triggered the thing off, and there was one hell of an explosion.'

'An explosion, Tim!'

'It was what they call a letter-bomb, although it was a bit bigger than that. There was a lot of rough and ready tidying up to do, not to speak of a very promising young fire to put out. Hat had been blown to shreds and was very messy. And there wasn't even a patch of garden to bury him in. So I scraped him into a bucket, and prowled around until I found a rubbish bin in the basement and nobody looking. *Requiescat in pace* Hat.'

Tim had gone very pale during the latter part of this fantastic recital, and his uncle wondered whether he himself had been doing so too. To have a domestic pet stand in for one, as it were, upon so naked a lethal occasion was a very unpleasant circumstance indeed. And it was no longer possible to suspect Tim of being a little wrong in the head. He had told the simple truth of the

98

incident – or at least the simple truth as he saw it.

'And what did you do then?' Averell asked. He had to make an effort to steady his voice.

'I sat down and gave the matter some thought.' Tim seemed to manage this cool reply without difficulty and with no attempt at bravado. 'It certainly required it.'

'But surely you ought to have–' But Averell checked himself; it was just no good talking to his nephew about the police. The boy wasn't fanatical about the police; he called them the fuzz and not the pigs; but they were wholly out of court with him, all the same. 'Surely you ought to have had some idea,' Averell emended, 'of why this ghastly thing had happened. And mightn't it have been aimed at somebody else?'

'It was addressed to me, wasn't it?' Very commendably, Tim was patient before this lapse into futility on his uncle's part. 'Of course, it might have *got* somebody else. The fact that it was badly made or something, and exploded just because it fell on the floor, means that lots of people must have been at risk from the moment it was posted. As it was, it just killed a pampered cat. I suppose if it had got its intended victim people might have said it had just killed a pampered undergraduate. Everything's falling to bits, isn't it? With me and my like doing very nicely in the middle of it.'

This hinterland of feeling in Tim, peeping out with such definiteness for the first time, disturbed Averell very much; he had a dim vision of tens of thousands of Tims – female as well as male, no doubt – ridden by such feelings of guilt and powerlessness.

'But there I was,' Tim resumed with recovered calm, 'and with not a clue to whys and wherefores. Fortunately there were practical considerations to get cracking on. There was this commune thing, you see. With it being university vacation and all that, other chaps – perhaps with their girls, even – might turn up and find themselves in the line of fire, so to speak. For it already seemed pretty certain to me that the people who had it in for Tim Barcroft would have another go. They hadn't just been doing a scaring – off turn. And there was no very easy way of sending out warnings. For nobody much knows where anybody else is nowadays, do they?'

Averell found this a bizarre generalization, again speaking of matters unknown to him. So for the moment he held his peace.

'I could pin up a notice outside the flat,' Tim pursued evenly. 'But somebody might come and take it down the moment I went away. I could leave a big notice just inside the flat. But then they might booby-trap its front door. It's the kind of thing they do in

Northern Ireland.'

'Well, what about *that?*' It seemed to Averell that he had a cogent question to ask at last. 'Have you been active lately, Tim, in that area of political feeling?' He felt that he had stumbled upon a pedantic and absurd form of words, but the substance of his question was pertinent enough. 'One hears of people being chosen out as targets on the most terrifyingly marginal pretexts of that sort.'

'True enough. But I assure you, Uncle Gilbert, that I've been in nothing of the kind. Over there, I happen to feel it's their own business to sort themselves out. But it's possible that some misconception may have arisen, all the same. I was once walloped at my prep school when it was another brat that had flung the ink pellet or whatever.' The memory of this seemed for a moment quite to cheer Tim up.

'Well, to continue,' he said. 'That was attempted assassination number one. Now I come to number two. If you can stand this recital of my woes, that is.'

'Go on.'

'I decided I had to begin with Boxes. I had to ring up my mother and tell her I wouldn't be coming home. That seemed quite obvious.'

'I suppose it must have.'

'There's no telephone in the flat – nor

anything much else, either. It's not exactly an apartment in the luxury class, as you can guess. So I decided to go to the nearest telephone booth, which is at the end of the street. I can't pretend it was a very carefree stroll. They'd be waiting to see if I'd been killed, quite probably. One of the simpler logical inferences, that. Even an Oxford philosopher couldn't much sophisticate it.'

'I suppose not.' Tim's youth came home to Averell as he was presented with this not altogether relevant remark. He was still a boy who sat in lecture-rooms listening to whatever learned nonsense was around. 'So then?'

'So then I set out. Most of our street is taken up by a thing that I think is a bottle factory. You'd imagine bottles must be manufactured in darkness, since there's nothing but a long high blank wall. Funnily enough, I've sometimes thought of it as a good place for a scene in some sort of hunted man affair on the flicks. And that was what happened. Nerve yourself, Uncle Gilbert.'

'Don't be a fool, Tim.' Averell was conscious of a strong start of affection for his nephew, and of a sudden reassuring perception that he wouldn't readily give in. 'Do you mean that they came at you again straight away?'

'Just that. It's a very quiet street, and it

was deserted, so far as I could see. I made along it, and I wasn't addle-pated enough not to be feeling a shade grim. That's why, when I heard a car behind me, I looked over my shoulder. And there it was, coming at me pretty fast. Not precisely like a thunderbolt, of course, since the fellow had to calculate rather delicately. He'd no intention of killing himself as well. Just a glancing squashing blow, I imagine, like you might make at a fly on a windowpane, and he'd either remain mobile himself for a getaway, or be able to jump out uninjured and make off. It was what you might call a long moment. For there was absolutely nothing I could do.'

'Obviously not. A fly would have had a resource that was denied you.'

'And so would a flea.' Tim grinned at his uncle, aware that he had attempted a coolness of response he didn't feel. 'But, as it happened, it was all perfectly all right. The chap miscalculated shockingly, and went bang into the wall a clear three yards in front of me. He'd crumpled the whole front of the bloody thing, but he managed to scramble out. I stood and looked at him. Nothing else to do.'

'No, I suppose not.'

'Then he came at me, feeling for something inside his jacket. The curtain was about to fall, you might say, on an impromptu effect.

And then I saw, quite suddenly, that there *was* something else to do. The kind of desperate flying tackle you have to make when things are happening far inside your own twenty-five. I always hated rugger. But that was it. I hurled myself – which is the correct dramatic word – at his knees, and brought him down. And at the same moment there was a terrible noise. It was like the clangour of the angel's trumpet and the horror of the ringing bell. John Donne. Actually, it was nothing but an ambulance in a hurry in the next street. I was still quite alone in a punch-up with this undesirable gent. But panic ensued – with him, I mean, since mine had somehow abated. He broke free, scrambled to his feet, and bolted. I was simply left with no other company than that smashed-up car.'

'And then?' Dear old Uncle Gilbert was conscious of having drawn a long breath.

'And then? Oh, I went on to the telephone kiosk and did my stuff. Not quite an alpha performance, I'm afraid, since my mother seemed to pick up that there was something mildly amiss. But I'd done my best.'

'So you had, Tim. But I'm worried about your feeling that it has all been something to keep under your hat.'

'Or Hat's hat. Well, yes – but there it is. And I'm worried too. Chiefly, I just felt I had to find out what it was all in aid of. I needed a bit of time to think. So I sent a telegram to the only chap whose address I knew – wrapping the thing up a bit, but saying the flat was over to him. Then I went into hiding for a time: a kind of one-man think-tank, you might say. That was probably a mistake. For I got the silly notion about kidnapped Barcrofts into my head, and came home after all. It wasn't clear thinking in the least. And there was a fat slice of funk to it. But I did have from the first, you know, the idea of getting my mother out of the country as well as the girls. And at least we've cleared the decks. And there's a bonus in that "we", Uncle Gilbert. Your turning up has been a bit of luck.'

'I hope it has, Tim.' As Gilbert Averell said this there came into his head the grotesque circumstances that the person to have turned up at Boxes was carrying the passport of an aristocratic Frenchman. It was a freakish thing virtually without significance in the light of what he was now faced with. But Tim ought to be told about it, all the same.

'As a matter of fact–' he began. And then any speech he might have made was interrupted by a fresh turn in the affair.

10

There had come a knock at the front door of Boxes. It was the common method by which visitors declared themselves, since a bell of antique type, operated by yanking at a dangling wire, had long since passed out of commission. But this knock had been a double knock, vigorously delivered, and Averell's first thought was that it signalled the arrival of the police. Perhaps they were after Tim or perhaps they were after the Prince de Silistrie. Averell was aware that the latter conjecture, at least, was implausible. He was thrown into considerable confusion, all the same.

Tim's mind moved differently, as was evident from his making an immediate grab at his gun. He knew nothing about Georges (now happily in Gubbio or some such Umbrian retreat) and it was hardly probable that he was going to point the thing at PC Capper, whom he had once been obliged so to embarrass as a young gentleman mysteriously on bail. Tim clearly thought that here were the assassins once more. Banging on the door was just a new technique on their part. It wouldn't be called a particularly novel one. Quite regularly nowadays one heard of some unfortunate victim of political enthusiasm opening his door to strangers and being shot dead on the spot.

'Tim,' Averell said urgently, 'I know what's in your mind, and conceivably you're right. So I'll open the door – being somebody they're not interested in – while you stand to the side and hold me covered with that thing. Right?'

This speech, which had taken them both into the hall, was astonishing in itself, since it revealed in a mild and elderly scholar what could only be called a lurking Bulldog Drummond mentality. Automatically you do the courageous and completely bone-headed thing, and all is well. But it was also astonishing in its result. Tim simply nodded, and took up an appropriate stance. This made of him a kind of well-trained Bulldog Drummond puppy, instant in obeying a command. Gilbert Averell possessed, it seemed, a good whack of authority, after all.

He unlocked and unbolted the door, and pulled it open. His first, and utterly confused, impression was that Kate and Gillian had returned to Boxes. Then he saw that the two young women on the doorstep were not in the least like his nieces. It was possible that they belonged to the same effete social class; but, if so, they had adopted a different style of life. Their attire vaguely suggested to him the sort of teenage females who squat outside little tents at pop festivals in commandeered parks. Yet they bore what might be called a businesslike appearance as well. They wore heavy walking boots, and each carried an enormous rucksack on her back. And now one of them stared first at Averell, and then over his shoulder, and then with a practised movement slid her burden to the ground.

'Hullo, Tim,' she said.

'Hullo, Anne.' It was in a noticeably sheepish manner that Tim returned this greeting, and as he did so he dropped the shotgun in an absurdly furtive manner into an umbrella stand.

'This is Lou,' Anne said.

'Hiyah, Tim,' Lou said.

'Hiyah, Lou,' Tim returned obediently. He added, 'This is Gilbert.'

'Hiyah, Gilbert.'

'Hullo, Gilbert.'

'I mean,' Tim said, like a man in desperation, 'that this is my uncle, Mr Averell.'

'How do you do?' Averell said – and almost added, 'I mean, hiyah.' Oddly enough, these muddled salutations rather pleased him. He was conscious in himself of a desire to appear by no means 'square' if he could manage it.

'Come along in,' Tim said. 'There's just Uncle Gilbert and me. My mother and sisters have gone abroad. I'll get you some

Nescafe or something.'

'We could do with a cuppa,' Lou said cheerfully. 'We had one good hitch with a commercial character, but did a fair deal of walking as well.'

The augmented company went into the drawing-room, and Tim made off hospitably to the kitchen. Anne, who appeared more at home in these surroundings than Lou, gave Averell a further appraising glance, and then wasted no time.

'Has Tim told you about recent events?' she asked crisply.

'Yes.'

'Tim sent a telegram to a man called Dave, and we had a get-together and think-it-out. Lou and I haven't seen the flat, but Dave and two other of the men have had a look at it. It's all a bit obscure, isn't it? We decided I'd hunt Tim down and get better genned-up. And Lou was to come too, because she'd be objective. Lou hasn't ever met Tim before.'

'Of course, I've heard about him,' Lou said. 'But only just as everybody has.'

'I see.' Averell was impressed at thus finding himself the uncle of a youth apparently credited with universal fame. 'I think it unfortunate,' he added firmly, 'that Tim has a thing about the police.'

'You have to respect convictions,' Lou said with an equal firmness. 'Even if it's a hung-up sort of attitude. And is it? I don't know. I'm open minded. I believe you can run up against a tolerably straight copper every now and then.'

'Ah, yes.' Averell didn't find this handsome admission encouraging. 'But you must not think I am lacking in respect for my nephew. That is far from being the case.'

'I'm sure it is,' Anne said. 'But let's stick to the point. We have to find a background to this. What has Tim been doing that could result in anybody having it in for him in a murderous way? We get nowhere without discovering that.'

Tim now returned with mugs of his instant coffee, and Anne got to work on him at once.

'About the bomb first,' she said. 'Did it injure you?'

'I didn't get a scratch. It killed the cat.'

'What about material damage?'

'Well, it's not beyond what one can clear up and make good, I suppose, so far as the landlord is concerned. But there was a fair amount of our own stuff damaged. Mostly mine, as it happens. My typewriter was on the table where the bomb was, and my camera and other photographic bits and pieces. All that's in smithereens. It's really rather annoying.' Tim paused on this surprisingly mild expression of feeling. 'And a lot of my lecture notes and essays pretty well soaked in poor Hat's blood.'

'Can you read them still?' Lou asked sharply. She appeared to be a girl of practical mind.

'Oh yes – I suppose so. But it's rather revolting.'

'I'd have them photocopied, if you feel that way. The copies wouldn't look so gruesome. You might think the stuff had just fallen into your bath or something while you were working on them.'

'I don't work in my bath,' Tim said. 'Do you?'

'Never tried it. Just stick to my bath toys, Tim.'

It seemed to Averell that, during this exchange of pointless quips, Tim was stirred to more interest in Lou, who was a stranger to him, than in Anne, whom he seemed to know well. Libidinous impulses, Averell seemed to remember, were natural and frequent in young men. But there is a time for everything, and he hoped that, in the present exigency, Tim wasn't going to be so frivolous as to take time off for amatory episodes. It was something that regularly happened in sensational fiction, particularly of a transatlantic sort. But he had a strong feeling, possibly irrational, that at Boxes it wouldn't be at all the thing. And was Lou particularly attractive as a sexual object? Was she more attractive than, say, Anne?

Finding himself pondering this totally irrelevant question surprised Averell. So did the disturbing discovery that he could himself arrive at no opinion on the matter. Senescence, he gloomily felt, must lie dead ahead of him.

'But your camera, Tim!' Ann was exclaiming in dismay. 'It was an enormously expensive one, wasn't it?'

'Well, yes – it was.' Tim said this a little awkwardly, perhaps because the camera had been a present from Uncle Gilbert on his twenty-first birthday. 'It's insured, though.'

'Do you always make people laugh?' Lou asked, with every appearance of candid surprise. 'If you want to keep this bomb to yourself, I expect people will say you must have your way, since it was you who was intended to be at the receiving end of the affair. But an insurance company will want to see the camera before they stump up. And when you hand it to them looking like a present from Hiroshima they'll ask the reason why. You must be joking.'

This cogent speech upset Tim a good deal – and (Averell felt) further heightened the boy's interest in the speaker. It would be a secure guess that the modest son-of-the-house at Boxes enjoyed the devotion of numerous young women in the circle in which he moved. The girl called Anne was one of them. Lou had not yet signed on.

And that was why some higher command in the commune, or whatever it was, had sent Lou – the objective Lou – along. She'd take a dispassionate look inside Tim's head and report on what was cooking there.

'But not all the recent photographs themselves?' Anne was asking with deepened horror. 'The demo in Parliament Square, and the mounted fuzz in Whitehall, and the ones that are to be for "Sitters-in at Home" in *En Vedette*, and all those racists marching in Notting Hill?'

'The whole lot,' Tim said, a shade impatiently. 'I had to put out a bit of a fire, you know, as well as coping with Death-and-Gory Hat. It doesn't matter a damn. There's plenty more of all that on the conveyor belt to do the candid camera on. And plenty of kids ready to take on the job. Thinking of themselves as investigative journalists uncovering all Hades in Pimlico. As for me, it's about time I was moving on and concentrating on something sensible. Housing, perhaps. I've been thinking a lot about that.'

It was evident that this was a rather scandalous speech – even a subversive one. It was Lou who took it in her stride.

'Glamour-boy's divine discontents are fine,' she said, 'and let them have their day. But the question seems to be whether he has all that many days to look forward to himself. Are they going to go on trying to kill you? It may be a petty question, but we're quite seriously interested in it.'

'All right. And yes, they are. They've been on the job down here at Boxes already.' For the moment Tim was really angry. 'Oddly enough, I'm quite seriously interested in that myself.'

Averell, who felt it would be imprudent to take any part in this spirited conversation, found himself not quite sure about the accuracy of what Tim had just said. In fact, there was really no evidence that the intruder of the previous afternoon and night had been lethally disposed. Of course he might have been. But equally he might have been less an intending assassin than a mere spy. Had the people who certainly had intended to kill Tim, and who had contrived two singularly brutal shots at it, for some reason changed their ground? Was there now something they simply wanted to *know* before they returned to one form or another of drastic action? And when one came to recall the matter coolly did not one feel that the interloper at Boxes had lacked the stuffing of, say, the man who had driven that car murderously at Tim in London? Certainly the episode in the dark showed up in retrospect as faintly ludicrous. A punch on the nose and a hack at the shins failed to add up to the behaviour to be expected of an atrocious criminal.

'Come right back,' Anne said. 'People suddenly wanting to liquidate Timothy Barcroft of Boxes Esquire. Just *why?* What have you been up to, Tim? I ask you.'

'I haven't a clue. Uncle Gilbert knows that.'

'Christ, Tim! You must know what you've been *doing*, mustn't you? Don't you keep a diary or something?'

'Certainly not. It's a most immature and conceited thing to do – keeping a diary.'

'*I* keep a diary,' Lou said. 'What about the funny little pocket diary all Oxford undergraduates are always peering at? Don't you even put engagements in it?'

'Never been engaged, Lou. But stay around, and I'll think it over.'

It was at least in some absence of mind, Averell noted, that Tim had produced this singularly undistinguished pleasantry. He was no longer casting any sort of speculative eye over the latest girl to arrive on his scene, but was scowling discontentedly into his coffee mug.

'Would I be in a state of shock?' he suddenly asked nobody in particular. 'It's something one's always reading about in the newspapers nowadays. You see your dear old grandmother fall downstairs and break her neck, and they take you to hospital and treat you for shock. Or you forget everything leading up to that terrible moment of granny's end, and that's called amnesia.'

'It's called anterograde amnesia, to be precise,' Lou said rather in the manner of an alert tutor. 'Go on.'

'Or you bolt into hiding as well – and for good measure fail to carry any notion of your own identity with you. At least I haven't succumbed to that. I'm Tim Barcroft.'

'But Tim,' Anne asked, 'is this in aid of anything? You're obviously none of these things.'

'Are you sure? *I'm* not sure. I may have forgotten *something,* don't you think? In fact, it almost looks as if I must have. It's very puzzling.'

At this point Averell felt he must chip in. He had remained silent for so long that he might be thought to be disapproving of this whole conference. It was true that its tone at times puzzled or even offended him. But he did feel that something might come of it.

'It mightn't be a bad idea,' he said, 'if Tim just tried to jot down a day to day record of his doings over the past week or so. I don't believe in his having forgotten anything – or not anything in the least memorable. But the point may lie just there.'

'How d'you mean, Uncle Gilbert?' Tim asked swiftly – and with an intentness which made Averell uncomfortably aware that a good deal was expected of him.

'I mean that one interpretation of the thing is this: that you may have come by information so unremarkable in itself that your mind sees, so to speak, no point in recalling it. But somebody else knows you have it, and is determined at all costs that it won't leak out and spread abroad.'

'Or be exploited,' Lou said, 'for purposes of blackmail. Something like that.'

'Lou!' Anne said indignantly. 'Are you saying that anybody could possibly imagine Tim turning into a blackmailer? Surely–'

'Lou obviously isn't saying that,' Averell interrupted pacifically. He was realizing that these young women were by no means bosom friends. 'But I can conceive myself believing that somebody was thinking of having a go at blackmail with me – provided I was sufficiently deeply of a criminal turn of mind myself. The wicked are wary, and the malevolent see malevolence all around them.'

'But it's quite absurd!' Anne said. 'About us, I mean.' For the moment, Anne wasn't thinking very clearly.

'It's a strange idea, certainly, Anne. But it's not to be rejected out of hand. Here's an absolute mystery still, and we need to hold on to every blessed idea we can grab by the tip of the tail.'

'Agreed,' Lou said firmly. 'Tim?'

'Well, yes. But how on earth could I come

by information leading straight into the area of murder and all that without myself having the remotest notion I was doing so?'

'That's where your day to day activities come in, Tim.' Averell paused for a moment. 'I admit it may be like looking for the needle in the haystack. But if there's a needle there it *can* be found – provided one looks hard and long enough.'

'And knows a needle when one sees it,' Lou said. 'The rub is there.'

'Perfectly true, Lou.' Averell paused for a moment's thought. 'Take a hypothetical case. Tim is sitting in a tube train, and a man comes in and sits down opposite to him. Tim for some reason studies this man in rather a thoughtful and covert-seeming way. Then Tim happens to open a briefcase and glance through a file of those famous photographs. He's shy and protective about his photographs for one reason or another. So it's rather obtrusively that he takes this peep at them in what he thinks is an unobtrusive way. Then he tucks them away again – and the man sitting opposite him simply isn't in his head. But *he* is in the man's head, all right. The man believes he has been identified. So at the next station he follows Tim – now thought of, let's say, as a sort of secret agent – up into the street and manages to shove him under a bus.'

'Thank you very much, Uncle Gilbert,'

118

Tim said rather wanly. 'A least it's a quick end.'

'It's a good *schema*,' Lou said. 'Of course, one could think up no end of other *schemata* to fit.' Lou, like the Barcroft twins, appeared to be vocabulary-conscious. She had been attending lectures, it was to be supposed, on the theory of art – or perhaps just on Immanuel Kant. 'And as a needle,' she added more colloquially, 'that man in the tube would be a hard nut to crack.'

Tim had now possessed himself of pencil and paper. It was evident that he had a considerable capacity for doing whatever his uncle suggested.

'I'll try to work backwards to the beginning of the month,' he said. 'I'm sure it would be no go after that. I've a rotten memory. I know it as often as I look at all my bloody notes on my reading. And I believe there's a theory that memory and intelligence are just different names for the same thing. It's discouraging.'

'There's hypnotism,' Anne said resourcefully. 'All sorts of memories can be recovered that way. Even of being born, they say.'

'Or conceived, I suppose.' Lou said this rather tartly. 'Or in the night of our fore-being or the Platonic *anamnesis*. All hooey. It makes me tired.'

'And there's the association of ideas,' Anne went on unheedingly. 'We just say things to Tim, and he makes spontaneous responses, and random recent memories are recovered that way.'

'I'm going to wash up,' Lou said. And she collected the coffee mugs and found her way to the kitchen.

Tim scribbled, bit his free thumb, scribbled, swore softly, scratched his head. Anne sat back and appeared to be according all these activities an equal respect. Averell sat back too. He had only a very little faith in the fruitfulness of the procedure he had suggested. And he was uneasy at his going along with these young people as he appeared to be doing. They weren't dealing with some harmless scrape but with a couple of gravely criminal acts which it was the duty of anyone aware of them to bring to the knowledge of the police. Not to do so was probably a crime in itself as well as a moral delinquency; perhaps it was what was called compounding a felony. That he had himself that trivial and stupid motive for ducking the notice of the law added to his discomfort. If Tim's affair took some further and yet more disastrous turn and the whole story emerged into the light of day this particular aspect of it wouldn't look well.

But that, he supposed, was a selfish consideration. And there had grown up overnight a kind of unspoken assumption that he had agreed to play the thing Tim's way and Tim's friends' way. He was steadily being admitted to more of their confidence on that understanding. It was an exceedingly awkward dilemma.

'Do you know?' Tim said, suddenly looking up from his task. 'This employment would be a salutary discipline to recommend to anybody.' He paused, and then glanced at Anne. 'Anne,' he said, 'run along and help Lou scratch up something for lunch. We've got to eat, after all.'

'Okay, Tim.' Anne got up and departed as obediently – Averell thought – as if she were Milton's Eve being banished while Adam held colloquy with a superior being. It suggested that even among the emancipated young certain of the old tyrannies of sexual subjugation prevailed at a pinch.

'Chronicles of wasted time,' Tim said. 'And worse. Here's no more than a fortnight – and a couple of exploits it just wouldn't do to bruit abroad in the old home. How disgusting!'

'Relevant exploits?'

'Who can tell? But I think not. Anyway, I'll put them on the reserve list. And here goes. So just listen, Uncle Gilbert.'

But again there was an interruption. This time, it was a ringing telephone bell.

11

Tim left the room to take the call. The telephone at Boxes was kept in a triangular cubby-hole under the staircase – Ruth having at some time had the very proper thought that young people ought to command a certain degree of privacy when using it. But this meant switching on a light, pulling a door to behind one, and crouching in a space which might have been deliberately designed as incommodious in a mediaeval dungeon. And all this was so heavy with conspiratorial suggestion that nobody would have thought of employing it, and thus all telephone conversations, however intimate, were cheerfully carried on *coram populo*. Through the open drawing-room door, therefore, Gilbert Averell heard snatches of this one. It was mostly a matter of Tim's listening to what was being said to him. His responses, as well as being monosyllabic in the main, were couched, it seemed to his uncle, in tones of mounting indignation. Tim said 'Good God, the swine!' and 'Utterly illegal, if you ask me' and 'Of course it would have to be by injunction, you bloody oaf!' Several times (and at this Averell's heart sank) he uttered the word 'Fuzz' preceded by an unprintable adjective (or at least one that Averell would not have put in print himself). 'Of course I'll come back at once!' he was eventually heard to say. Then he banged down the receiver, emerged from the cupboard, and shouted unceremoniously through the house at large.

'Hi!' Tim shouted. 'Anne – and you, what's-your-name. Come here at once.'

Thus rudely apostrophizing a young woman with the perfectly respectable name of Lou was on Tim Barcroft's part an indication that he was exceedingly upset. So Averell was prepared for disaster as the boy stormed into the drawing-room again and his guests hurried across from the kitchen to join him.

'That was Dave,' Tim said more quietly. He had turned very pale, but it was impossible to tell whether this was from indignation or dismay. 'He got away. It doesn't sound as if any of the others did.'

'What do you mean – got away? Got away from where?' It was Anne who, round-eyed, asked the questions. She had perhaps never seen Tim like this before.

'From the Uffington Street Squat – the one I was covering for *En Vedette*. It's an outrage. The fuzz broke in on them and yanked them out – without so much as brandishing a warrant or a summons or an injunction from some dotty old judge or what-have-you. Yanked them out, and now they're all inside.'

'Inside?' Lou said. 'Inside where?'

'Those bloody little white-washed cells, I suppose. With hulking great brutes standing round them and telling them to say this and that. It's monstrous. It was a perfectly legal squat.'

'Can squats be perfectly legal?' Averell asked. He knew that he was on singularly unfamiliar ground.

'The next thing to it,' Tim said – this time a shade uncertainly. 'I've got up the law. We've all got up the law. They could only be proceeded against individually and by name and as a matter of civil trespass and all that. But the police have thought up something quite fantastic. They've been told they'll probably be charged with robbing a bank.'

Very reasonably, this produced a moment's stupefied silence. It had to be broken by Averell.

'Friends of yours, Tim?' he asked mildly.

'Of course they're friends of mine. Not that I've known many of them for long. Only since last week, most of them. But they certainly don't rob banks.'

'I suppose not.' Averell wished he could feel confident about this. In circles frequented by his nephew it wasn't inconceivable that there were young people who judged banks to be thoroughly iniquitous institutions, and bankers no better than robbers themselves. And he had no faith at all in the notion of a constabulary trumping up a charge of larceny against innocent young persons, however great the nuisance-value of their social or political persuasions. 'About this Uffington Street,' he said. '*Is* there a bank in it?'

'Of course there is, Uncle Gilbert.' Tim produced this reply in a tone of wholly unreasonable irritation. 'Two doors down from the house. I passed it several times when I was mucking in a bit with the Uffington Street crowd. But it just isn't–'

'Does your friend Dave know how this robbery is supposed to have been accomplished?'

'He's rather vague, but finding out what he can. The fuzz aren't uttering. I'm going back to London now to blast the lights out of them. You can all come. I'll ring up and hire a car.'

'We'd better have some sandwiches,' Lou said prosaically. 'I'll go fix them.' With this modish Americanism she followed Tim from the room. Averell and Anne were left staring at each other.

'This is unfunny,' Anne said. It was clear that she was much upset, so that Averell wondered whether keeping Tim out of mischief was at present her main task in life. 'Let's go into the garden, shall we?'

'Yes, if you like.' Averell stood up at once.

It looked as if Anne might have something to say in confidence about this new and bewildering development. With this in his head, Averell quite forgot the nonsense about Boxes being in a state of siege. And it certainly proved pleasant to be out of doors. There had been a shower during the earlier part of the morning; now the sun was shining; there would be another shower soon. France, it seemed to Averell, or at any rate Paris, didn't ever run to this quintessentially April-like effect. The earth was gently steaming, and so was Smoky Joe – just as if he were obligingly disposed to justify his name. Anne, who was presumably exploring the place for the first time, led the way between roughly trimmed box hedges towards a tumbledown summerhouse.

'Don't the Barcrofts take a newspaper?' she asked.

'I don't think they do. My sister is rather fond of keeping a little clear of the world.'

'One can't say that of Tim.'

'I suppose not. And I admire his power to get concerned about things.'

'What I was thinking of, Mr Averell, is that this affair must be in the papers today.'

'The arrest of those young people?'

'Well, no. That might be sat on for a bit. But the actual bank raid, or whatever it has been. These things seem to be reported fairly quickly. Not that they're not a bit two-a-penny nowadays.'

'I suppose they are. In fact I noticed something in a paper yesterday that seemed to be speaking of them in general as quite that. I'm afraid I don't often actually read about such things.'

'They come in various shapes and sizes. Sometimes crooks simply dash into a bank waving guns, and grab what they can and depart again. Fairly primitive, that – and not likely to result in a big haul. Then there's the trick of hiding in the place overnight, and pouncing on some wretched understrapper when he opens up in the morning. And, of course, there's all sorts of stuff with hostages. It's astonishing what you can do with an advanced technique there. Make the manager drive up with the keys in his shiny car, and depart in the shiny car yourselves when you've cleared the place out. But then it's fifty-fifty there will be a chase, and when that happens the odds are on the police.' Anne paused in this well-informed discourse to admire some primroses. 'But the really superior method is tunnelling. You start from, say, an empty shop near by; keep on burrowing and burrowing like a mole; and if you emerge at the right spot all you have to do is turn the key deftly in the oiled wards. I think Keats or somebody put it that way.'

'He well may have. But are you saying,

Anne, that this affair has probably been like that?'

'Yes, I am – and that when the police got into the bank's vault or whatever it was, and worked back through the tunnel, they found themselves in the middle of this idiotic squat. So they naturally nicked everybody they could lay their hands on.'

They had reached the summerhouse, which faced into the sun. Anne dusted down a bench as carefully as if she had been in a ball-dress, and perched herself on it.

'Romantic seclusion,' she said, 'but I'm not expecting a declaration. Sit down too, Mr Averell, and tell me what you think.'

'I think you may well prove to be right.' Averell sat down as he was bidden, although not without a fear that the bench might be a little damp. 'But it doesn't take us far with what we have really to think about.'

'Which is just what connection all this has with people wanting to kill Tim? There must be a connection, I suppose.'

'I'd rather imagine so. But I'm not at all clear about his role, Anne. He doesn't seem to have been particularly closely connected with this squat – if that's what it's called. Was he simply going to do a report on it?'

'More or less that – though mostly it would have been his photographs. And it was just to be part of a series. The idea was to show squatting and sitting in and so forth in the rather domestic and civilized way it usually happens. People get the impression that squatters pee on the carpet, and get drunk and quarrel, and end by breaking everything up. So there was to be lots of good humour and co-operative effort and listening to Bach as well as pop. It was to be a public relations exercise of sorts. Say a counter-blast to the media.'

'I see. And Tim mayn't really have known all that much about this particular crowd?'

'No, he needn't. And I don't know how often he went round there. I haven't been hearing an awful lot about his movements lately, as a matter of fact.'

Averell considered this for a moment in silence. He had already been wondering whether perhaps Tim didn't care about Anne as much as Anne cared about Tim. He resolved to steer clear of this if he could. It decidedly wasn't territory upon which an elderly relation could trespass to any good effect.

'Just before that telephone call came,' he said, 'Tim seemed about to give me the results of a kind of diary of his recent movements. But I didn't get the impression he'd recalled anything significant. The real puzzle, in a way, is his being so puzzled.'

'Yes, something must have happened without his realizing its significance – like what you said about a man in a tube train.

When he was being a bit dopey, perhaps.'

'Dopey?' Averell repeated, alarmed.

'No, no – just being dreamy. Would you say Tim was rather thick?'

'Certainly not.' Averell found himself resenting this sudden sharp question. 'It is the general expectation at Oxford that Tim will take a most creditable degree.'

'Wouldn't that be super?' Anne asked ironically. But it was evident that she was pleased. 'If he ever gets as far as the examination room,' she said. 'But remember that they do have it in for him. They may really put him in prison this time.' As she faced this dire possibility, Anne broke most unexpectedly into tears.

Averell was appalled. He would have been distressed merely by the bobbing up once more of the shocking notion that the police could 'have it in' for his nephew. But to have a young woman weeping on his bosom in a secluded situation was infinitely alarming. And it was on his bosom. Quite instinctively he had put an arm round the weeping girl in what he judged vaguely to be an avuncular manner, and she had promptly responded by burying her nose in the region of his breast-pocket handkerchief.

'My dear Anne–' he began – and suddenly stiffened and straightened up. From somewhere close at hand, in fact from just outside the summerhouse, had come a most alarming sound. It was the sharp *click!* surely to be associated (Averell thought) with the cocking of a pistol, if pistols are in fact things one does cock. He was uncertain about this – but in no doubt of the resurgence of what a writer of romance might entitle *Peril at Boxes*. Here was the enemy again: the prowler of the previous afternoon, the intruder at the bedroom window, the ruffian who had so outrageously bashed him on the nose. And Averell's duty was plain. Standing as he did the sole protector of the girl at his side from an assailant who might be sheerly mad, it was his duty once more to grapple with him as he could. Averell disengaged himself from Anne (who was a little bewildered and unwilling to let go), sprang to his feet, and undauntedly dashed from the summer-house. And at this Anne for some reason decided that it was her duty to follow, so that the two tumbled out of the place almost together. It was at once evident that the miscreant was not meditating a more effective attack, since he was in fact plainly visible retreating rapidly down the garden path. Perhaps, Averell resourcefully thought, that click had been the sound made by a pistol when it goes abruptly out of working order. At least the man was now a fugitive. And he was to be pursued.

The man ran, Averell ran, and Anne ran too. Anne, ashamed of her moment of womanly weakness, was showing herself a tough girl. She was still at Averell's shoulder when Averell caught up with his quarry. This he succeeded in doing only because the fugitive made a mistake, turning down a path that proved to be a blind alley. Unless he showed fight and got the better of the encounter, he was cornered at last! Averell, whose blood was up, had no intention of being worsted.

But now the fugitive, realizing that he could no further go, halted and turned round. Averell halted too, and even more abruptly. For here was none other than Monsieur Gustave Flaubert, his vexatious acquaintance of the flight from Paris. And Flaubert, as if making the best of things, was entirely composed. He was wearing his silly little hat of the previous day, and this silly little hat he now elevated in air, while at the same time making a courteous bow.

'Bonjour, Monsieur le Prince,' Flaubert murmured (as one might to an acquaintance in the Champs Elysées, or some such place). And he glided past Averell's shoulder and walked collectedly away.

'Just what was that in aid of, Mr Averell?' Anne asked. 'I'm sorry that I turned so sappy, by the way.'

'It was only natural,' Averell said – much at random. 'And – well, I thought I heard him doing something to a gun.'

'You heard him doing something with a camera. He had it slung over his shoulder when we came up with him now. But I don't understand this at all. He seemed to know you. Is that right? And then you seemed to feel that the sooner he just cleared out the better.'

'I encountered him on an aeroplane yesterday. He is a most annoying person, and I certainly never want to see him again.'

'He called you something funny, Mr Averell.' Anne was looking at Tim's uncle with momentary frank suspicion. 'Only I didn't quite catch it.'

'He called me *Monsieur le Prince*.' Averell came out with this quite firmly.

'And are you a prince? Nobody told us, if you are. Of the Holy Roman Empire or something?'

'Certainly not.' Averell positively snapped this out, since he had in fact become extremely embarrassed. 'It is an absurd affair of mistaken identity, which it would take too long to explain. I think we had better return to the house.'

'It has nothing to do with this bank robbery, and the attacks on Tim?'

'So far as I can see, nothing whatever.'

'Then why did he try to come at Tim last night in his bedroom?'

'He didn't. He had something quite different in view.' As he said this, Averell began to walk rapidly back to the house, somewhat ungallantly leaving it to Anne to follow if she chose. He hadn't quite worked it all out, but he had, as it were, got the idea. And to say another word about it now to this blameless child would just be too humiliating altogether.

PART TWO

UFFINGTON STREET
AND ELSEWHERE

12

There was more telephoning, as a result of which the young man called Dave drove out from London to a rendezvous with the party from Boxes at a 'service area' on the M4 near Heathrow. It was a species of amenity for travellers quite unfamiliar to Gilbert Averell, although it might have been described as a somewhat graceless first cousin to places of roadside refreshment into which he had occasionally been introduced in both France and Italy. There were acres of parked cars, and further acres of coaches, and yet further acres of transport Juggernauts. And there was a complex of wash-places both for automobiles and humans at the core of which was a further complex of cafeterias and snack-bars and a scurrying restaurant in which the air was pervaded equally by deplorable music and a clatter of crockery. Harassed men and women, mainly from distant quarters of the globe, swished out-size mops round your toes and swabbed down little tables under your nose; myriads of children howled for cokes and chips and fish fingers; brawny men gnawed pies.

Tim had dismissed their hired car before

making contact with Dave, and this, although a rational procedure, enhanced Averell's sense that he had implicated himself with conspiratorial young persons. And Dave himself was perplexing. Averell couldn't place him at all. His car was a large Bentley – a circumstance which, although it was of mature years, suggested a background of considerable substance. Again, although Dave's hairstyle and attire suggested what Averell thought of as a hippie (or was it a beatnik?) much more than did anything about Tim and the two girls, he seemed to be basically the sort of young man whose notion of professional activity includes becoming an officer in the Brigade of Guards. This small social enigma was no doubt of very little consequence. Tim and Anne, after all (although not perhaps Lou), were in strict class terms out of the same drawer as this young man – although he might be rich, and Tim at least had some title to call himself poor. A social mix up (in what Averell told himself were his own archaic and hide-bound terms) was clearly judged agreeable and edifying in the coteries with which Tim had involved himself.

They sat round an undersized table, drank an approximation to coffee, and ate the sandwiches which Lou had provided – together with several bags of crisps purchased on the spot. Averell, although not normally self-conscious, saw himself as awkwardly out of the picture. A fat woman at the next table kept staring at him in a wooden way. Almost certainly it was from no more than a kind of inert stupidity. But Averell actually found himself supposing that she was turning him over in her mind.

'I keep on thinking,' Dave said, 'that I know what all this is about. And then it eludes me.'

'And so do I, Dave.' Tim seemed instantly to recognize in Dave some mental process akin to his own.

'But Tim has what you might call the livelier interest,' Lou said crisply. 'They tried to murder him in or around the flat twice within an hour. And then they tracked him to Boxes too.'

'I don't think–' Averell began, and then fell silent. If he took up this point at all it would merely confuse matters by introducing something totally irrelevant to the alarming happenings in London. He had already said as much as this to Anne, and he saw no reason to regard it as untrue. (Time was very rapidly to reveal a small factor of error in this. But Averell, being unendowed with any precognitive faculty, was unaware of the fact.)

'But I believe I have got some way,' Tim was saying, 'in sorting the thing out. It's a matter, for a start, of the character of this takeover of the Uffington Street house. I went there two or three times, you know, on account of the photographs and all that, and it didn't strike me, somehow, as quite the usual thing.'

'Nor me,' Dave said.

'It wasn't going to make the public relations side of the job easy. Too few homeless chaps with wives and young kids to give the required key-note. The effect was more of a round-the-clock pop concert really. That's a very good thing in its way, but there in Uffington Street it was a bit of a racket. Of course people were smoking this and that, and demi-semi-concealing themselves when suddenly feeling affectionate. I did a bit in a candid-camera way, since it seemed to be expected of me.'

'Tim, how disgusting!' Anne said sharply.

'Oh, well – nothing exotic,' Tim said easily. 'And it isn't my point that there was a certain amount of wantoning and chambering. Have you ever been to a hunt ball, Anne – or something of that kind?'

'Yes, I have.'

'With me,' Dave said. 'Perhaps she has never told you, Tim. But Anne and I share a murky past in polite life.'

'Don't be silly, Dave.' Anne was clearly annoyed by this revelation. 'Tim, go on.'

'Well, you remember how there is always a photographer who snaps Mr *A* chatting with Lady *B*, and who huddles people into grinning groups all jollied up on caterers' champagne. I did quite a lot of that one night in Uffington Street. One or another clutch of chums, you know. So you all see what's in my head.'

'At any rate, I do.' Lou said. 'You believe yourself to have photographed the gang that did the bank robbery – and they woke up to the undesirableness of the fact rather late.'

'Just that, Lou. What a smart girl you are.'

'It seems to me wholly improbable,' Dave said. 'I grant you that in all that squatting crowd, and with all the coming and going there was, a little gang of professional thieves might lurk. But if they *were* professionals they certainly wouldn't line up smirking in front of the wonder-boy's candid lens.'

'It might depend on the champagne – or whatever was the equivalent of that.' Averell offered this contribution to the debate considerably to his own surprise. 'A mood of bravado may have overtaken them. Or they mayn't even have known at the time what was going on. They may have been alerted to it afterwards.'

'And decided to take care of the photographer,' Anne said. 'I suppose there *are* people as desperately wicked as that.'

'Oh, most certainly,' Dave said cheerfully. 'And there would be big stakes in this affair. Then there's another thing, and it makes me feel that perhaps Tim's on the right track, after all. There probably aren't all that many high-powered gangs able to tunnel their way into vaults and strong rooms. And at least some of them will be known already to the police. So if a crowd like that turned up in photographs taken by our young ace in Uffington Street, the fuzz would know just who they were looking for.'

'But would it be possible,' Averell asked, 'for even three or four men to gate-crash this squat, and be around perhaps for several days, and pass undetected? And it would have to be for several days, if they really had a big burrowing operation on hand. And I don't quite see how that could have been managed at all.'

'For a start,' Tim said, 'the squat was a gate-crashing operation itself, in a way. And people drifted away from it and others came in: that always happens in these affairs. And not everybody would be known to everybody else, by any means. And it's really a very big house, with cellars and attics and what have you. No, it all seems quite feasible to me.'

'What about the racket?' Lou asked. 'You can't bore your way–'

'Yes, you can.' Tim was confident. 'It sounds strange, and it must all be pretty laborious. But it's certainly possible to excavate long tunnels as quietly as if you were moles yourselves. People did it to escape from prison camps, and they do it today to get into banks and shops and offices. Not a doubt about that. And what made a real row in Uffington Street was all those groups.'

'Groups?' Averell said.

'Small bands, Uncle Gilbert. You might call a string quartet a group. Somebody brought one in, it seems, to brighten things up, and the idea caught on. There were visits from several more – for free, I imagine. One or two hung about for quite a long time.'

'True enough,' Dave said. 'I gave one of them a hand, as a matter of fact. Quite nice chaps, but there were two or three others I know nothing about. I say! Isn't a group much the same as a gang? There's our answer, I do believe.'

'But what about the answer thought up by the fuzz?' Anne asked. 'It's our business to do something about that.'

'I've an idea we ought to be thinking about the fuzz,' Averell said – and was displeased to hear himself use this presumably derogatory term. What he was now wondering, was whether these young people were inclined a little to discount the intelligence of the forces of the law. 'I mean,' he went on cautiously, 'that their minds may have been moving not altogether differently from our own. They may have seen the probability of professional criminals having mingled successfully with your squatting acquaintances, and may be detaining the whole lot simply in the hope that some process of sifting and identification may reveal the crooks as still lurking in the bag. In fact, I can't take the notion of a wholesale charge of bank robbery against the lot of them at all seriously.' Averell was gaining confidence as he spoke. 'But we can't really get very far without much more precise information than we seem to have. Have you any notion, Dave, of how the theft was discovered?'

'Oh, just as such things always are discovered. When the bank people arrived and opened up in the morning.'

'We seem to know how the robbers entered the bank. But how did they leave it?'

'By the same route, I imagine, it's probably not much easier to leave a locked up bank than to enter it. So they'd have retreated down their tunnel with their booty. But this is just what chaps are saying. The fuzz keep mum.'

'No doubt. And once the thieves were back on the squatters' ground they could slip away unobserved and more or less at once, even lugging their booty with them?'

'Well, not exactly staggering under crates of bullion, I suppose. But in a general way, yes. There would always be a lot of free coming and going, and nobody taking much notice. There was me, for instance. I was there overnight, but happened to leave very early in the morning. The police hadn't a cordon round the place, you know, simply because there were squatters in it. It would be quite illegal to try to prevent people going in and out.'

It didn't seem to Averell that much of this was very illuminating, and he wondered what plan of action, if any, was forming in his companions' minds. Their present surroundings he continued to find depressing. It was a long time, for one thing, since he'd eaten potato chips. And, for another, the fat woman was still staring at him. Or perhaps he was imagining this. Perhaps she was staring at each of them in turn. Did they look in any marked degree peculiar or out of the way? He had no idea.

'I haven't quite got hold of the timescale,' Lou was saying, 'except that we seem to be hearing about it all a bit belatedly. And, just like Gilbert, I come back to all those arrests.' (Averell was surprised but unoffended at hearing himself thus familiarly referred to.) 'If the thieves *could* walk out – just as Dave walked out – they *would* walk out. So the arrests were sheer unwarranted harassment. Somebody should ask a question about them in the House of Commons.'

'No good coming back to the bees in our own bonnets,' Tim said a little unexpectedly. 'The crooks might still have been lurking in the bag, as Uncle Gilbert says, when the police piled in and found the tunnel. I don't think that a charge that the fuzz had been high-handed would meet with much public sympathy. Particularly as everybody may well have been let go by now. It seems to me that our first job is to get clued up on just that.'

At this moment the fat woman (who was unaccompanied by any male escort) made a move, getting ponderously to her feet and waddling towards an exit. Her route took her past the table occupied by the party from Boxes, and as she came abreast of them she put out a hand and very impudently ruffled Dave's hair. Or that was the appearance of the thing. Dave, not unnaturally, was displeased. But, although pale with anger, he sat tight and did nothing – which was precisely what one would have expected (Averell reflected) of so evidently well-bred a young man. And it was only when the fat woman had vanished that Anne spoke.

'She's left something.' Anne said. 'Posted it, you might say.'

At this Dave ran his own hand through his hair, which was certainly sufficiently abundant for what had been the fat woman's purpose. It came away holding a small twist of paper, which he unrolled, studied briefly, and then handed round his companions. It bore a brief message, scrawled in pencil:

Get lost, Dirtylocks! Nose out, see? Or else...

To this succinct message a roughly sketched skull and crossbones had been appended by way of signature.

'Well, well!' Dave said, with what appeared to be genuine calm. 'My turn now. And rather like the Black Spot in *Treasure Island*. Who'd suppose an old soul like that to be of a literary inclination? Anne my dear, please rearrange my *coiffure* for me.'

Anne at once performed this service unaffectedly with a pocket comb. Neither she nor any of the others ventured to comment on the unfairness of the fat woman's derogatory appellation.

'Now we'll be moving,' Tim said briefly.

'Do we know where to?' Lou asked.

'To wherever we can find some of those squatters, for a start.' Tim was quite clear about this. 'Even if it's in quod. We need a lot more in the way of first-hand impressions of what went on. Even Dave was like me – only in on it in a marginal way, it seems.'

'Let's think about Dave now,' Lou said. 'About what has just happened, I mean. Why should those people add him to their death-list? *He* hasn't been taking photographs. Or if he has we haven't been told about it.'

'Never took a photograph in my life.' Dave said. 'It's a middle-class habit. A bourgeois habit, I mean.'

'And you *haven't* exactly been added to a death-list.' Tim said. 'They've just warned you off. It was me who was on a death-list. But they didn't tell me so. They just had a couple of goes at me straight away, and I pretty well expect another any minute. It may be said they've gone soft on Dave. I wonder why?'

'Perhaps because he's so adorable,' Lou said.

'Nonsense! I'm adorable too. Anne, aren't I adorable?'

'If you are, you're an idiot as well.' Anne was finding this gaiety unseasonable. 'And listen! Unless I've got it wrong, there's one big difference between Tim and Dave. Tim, just when did that letter-bomb thing arrive on you?'

'First post Monday.'

'Well, that's one fact. Dave, what about the break-in at the bank?'

'Oh, haven't I made that clear? I thought I told Tim on the blower. Tuesday in the small hours.'

'Exactly! And there's the difference between our two heroes. They try to kill Tim just *before* their robbery. And they start threatening Dave a couple of days *after* it. And just threatening. We still don't know what to make of that.'

'A branch of the gang,' Anne said, 'that

believes in milder courses than the lot who had a go at Tim.'

'I'm not exactly flattered.' Dave said this without any apparent humorous intention. 'It's rather a slight, really – as if I can be scared and Tim couldn't be. I wonder.'

This produced a moment's silence, and then Tim spoke robustly.

'Utter rot!' Tim said. 'And anyway, it remains true, broadly speaking, that the villains now have both of us on their shopping list.'

'I don't know that that is quite necessarily so.' Averell said this rapidly, conscious that for him a moment of truth had come. 'And, in order to explain what I mean, I'm afraid I must tell you about something extremely silly – and, in a way, totally irrelevant to this present business. I have a French friend called Georges.' Averell paused on this, aware that it sounded quite idiotic. 'Tim, I think you met him once when you were visiting me in Paris.'

'The prince chap, who's the split image of you, Uncle Gilbert?'

'Yes, that's right. And on this occasion, as it happens, I've come to England as him.'

'You've *what?*' Tim was goggling at his uncle. And so was everybody else – very much (Averell thought) as if he had suddenly been transmogrified into a two-headed calf.

'And he has gone off to Italy as me. It

hasn't been exactly a wager; rather what we used to call, when I was young, a dare.' Averell felt that he might decently soften the truth by sticking to this aspect of the thing. It was a genuine aspect in its way. 'And then something very odd seems to have happened. It's particularly odd since Georges isn't a married man.' Averell paused again, conscious that this trend in his attempted narrative was alarming his nephew a good deal. 'Somebody must have decided to have Georges followed – trailed or shadowed, that is, by the sort of person who is called a private enquiry agent.'

'Do you mean a private eye?' Lou asked.

'I suppose I do. And this one goes by the name – it's really quite preposterous – of Gustave Flaubert. He caught up with me on the plane from Paris, and in one way and another followed me to Boxes. Anne, you now understand a little about this, don't you? Because of what happened in the garden, I mean.'

'Do I? Yes, perhaps.' Anne sounded a shade grim. 'Just who could have hired this person?'

'I think it must have been a jealous mistress.' Averell was not at all sure that it was proper to admit to the existence of mistresses, jealous or otherwise, in the presence of young English gentlewomen. 'At first I thought that Georges was playing some sort of practical joke on me. He's quite capable of it. But it can't be that. It's some woman who hopes to have Georges detected in – well, in an alternative irregular situation.'

'With a rival tart, you mean?' Lou asked baldly.

'Just that. It was Flaubert, of course, who peered in at the drawing-room window soon after I arrived at Boxes. And who climbed up to my bedroom window in the night. He wasn't one of this gang, mistaking my room for Tim's, as Tim and I thought. He was really after me in what's called a compromising situation. There was a sudden blaze of light woke me up, and that I vaguely took to be lightning. But it was Flaubert having a go with a flashlight camera.'

'You mean,' Dave asked with wholesome amusement, 'that he hoped to snap you in bed, enarming a new mistress – "you" being, of course, supposed to be this prince person?'

'Yes, precisely that. It's all most disagreeable.'

'It's all bloody funny, if you ask me. Is there any more of it, Mr Averell?'

'Yes, there is.' It was Anne who broke in with this. She was probably conscious that in the regard of Tim's elderly uncle the most embarrassing aspect of the story was yet to come. 'The man *did* get a photograph – this morning. And he was so cheered that he put on an impudent turn on the strength of it. It so happened, you see, that Gilbert and I were sitting in a rather romantic arbour – or, at least, a summerhouse – and that I was blubbering on his shoulder, so that what Dave calls enarming was to be snapped for the asking. So Flaubert has his evidence that this prince man has skipped over to England for immoral purposes.'

'Well, well,' Dave said. 'And good on you, Anne.'

'I certainly agree that it's a thoroughly absurd story, Uncle Gilbert.' It was clear that Tim thought it distinctly unbecoming as well. 'It's the sort of thing that might happen to Mr Pickwick, or somebody like that. But I don't see that it has much to do–'

'God, Tim Barcroft, don't be so thick!' Dave exclaimed. 'The point of it is that you were not followed to Boxes. It was your uncle who was followed to Boxes. Get?'

'Yes, of course. But–'

'And that means there's no evidence that they've *added* me to you. They've *substituted* me for you. You're *passé*, chum – entirely old-hat. And why? Well, forget about this Flaubert and his photographs, and think about yours. The relevant hunt-ball group of this gang of crooks. And the whole lot you took at Uffington Street. Where are they now?'

'Where are they? In ashes, of course.

Everything photographic I possessed went west in that big bang and the healthy baby fire that followed.'

'Well, well, well. And did you hasten to tell anybody that?'

'No, I didn't. But I made a kind of inventory before I quit the flat and went home. I felt I was being businesslike in regard to the insurance, and so on. Only later I rather forgot about it. I must just have left it there.'

'Jesus Christ, Tim! Anybody can walk into that flat.'

'That's true.'

'These people now know the bomb didn't get you – nor the car either. But they also know the photographs were destroyed, and they're prepared to call it a day.'

'All right.' Tim managed a faint grin. 'With me they are. But now it's you.'

'And why, oh why?' Lou said. 'When we get that we get somewhere. Let's move.'

13

Perhaps because in France his acquaintance covered a fairly wide social spectrum (including characters like the Prince de Silistrie), Averell was not without experience of being driven furiously around in powerful cars. Even so, he was at times a shade alarmed by Dave's performance on the final stretch of the M4. Dave kept in the fast lane, and was far from patient when held up on it because a car in front of him was trundling along at the mere permitted maximum of seventy miles an hour. On these occasions his use of a powerful if melodious horn was more vigorous than a proper courtesy would have allowed. Dave was no doubt eager to get cracking at what they were going to take a crack at (whatever this might be, for the matter remained disturbingly obscure). But it was also possible to feel that Dave was being more venturesome than he would normally be because he judged that it was up to him to vindicate himself in some way. He had possibly been irked by Anne's little joke about the gang's supposing him to be vulnerable to 'milder courses' than those they had directed against Tim. Young men, after all, are very sensitive to any aspersion cast upon their courage. Anne, indeed, hadn't intended anything of the sort. It had been Dave himself who had twisted her remark that way. And this in itself was indicative. Averell made a mental note to try to keep a cautious eye on Dave. The boy might be prone to exhibit what a reader of Joseph Conrad would call the Lord Jim syndrome: to do a rash thing the moment an opportunity so to do turned up. Tim had been a little like this when he had insisted on wandering around the garden at Boxes waving a torch in face of what he had believed to be the possibility of lethal attack. Tim would be the more circumspect of the two young men, all the same. There was nothing particularly admirable about circumspection in itself. But it was to be commended, surely, when one happened to be toting around a couple of young women in the interest of running to earth a band of atrocious criminals.

These thoughts did credit to Gilbert Averell as an elderly person of chivalrous disposition. At the same time he was aware that he might more profitably be addressing his mind to something else: namely, to finding some persuasive means of bringing the entire freelance operation within the ambit of the law. But this was difficult, since all four of his companions were in the grip of another syndrome which might reasonably be associated with the name of Robin Hood. They were a band of jolly outlaws, intent on righting wrong without any recourse to a Sheriff of Nottingham or his latter-day equivalent in, say, an office at Scotland Yard.

Could he venture to tell them that they were in a muddle? They clearly had no strong feelings about a large-scale depredation visited upon a bank. Dave (rushing around in his expensive car) was probably quite capable of asserting roundly that all property was theft, and that if anybody lost out as a result of the raid (and it was the paradoxical truth that nobody in the world would at all intimately do so) it served them right for hoarding wealth that ought to be common to all. (This was a highly speculative assumption on Averell's part, since in fact he knew little about either the minds of young people in general or the minds of the particular batch of young people with whom chance had so oddly implicated him.) What really commanded Tim and his friends was the sense that a harmless section of society – to wit, persons deprived of homes through no fault of their own – had been pounced on by the police and huddled off to unwarranted incarceration. Averell found he couldn't very readily associate himself with this feeling – or not if, as he judged probable, this had been a temporary measure now liquidated. If one 'squatted' one couldn't very reasonably resent certain occasional inconveniences to result.

But this was a persuasion which he could not perhaps without indiscretion admit to. And there was, of course, the absurd fact that, within the Queen's realm, he was at the moment something of an outlaw himself. He hadn't honestly admitted to this. He had fudged the full facts of his present embarrassing and unseemly position. So he now found himself cursing his wholly agreeable friend Georges' fantastic sense of fun.

'We'll drive straight to Uffington Street,' Dave said, 'and see if any of the wretches have been allowed to return there. Tim, you agree?'

'Yes, of course.' But as Tim said this he had glanced for a moment at his uncle, as if from a sense that the senior member of the party ought to have been consulted first. This unthinking impulse of deference merely served to make Averell yet more ill at ease in his anomalous position, and he rather wished that he had stayed put at Boxes and left these four young people to their adventure. But had he done so he would immediately have felt himself to be irresponsibly deserting them. Or he would have felt this had he not contacted the police the moment they had driven off; and that was something they would have regarded as plain treachery. There was nothing for it but to bear his part. So he spoke up again now.

'Will any of them have been let go back to this empty house?' he asked. 'Even, I mean, when they've been entirely cleared of having anything to do with the robbery. I'd suppose that once squatters were out they'd be kept out. Or at least that the owner of the place would come along and bar it all up.'

'It's the law again, Uncle Gilbert,' Tim said – and with his customary air of being an authority on this subject. 'The various forms of trespass are extremely dodgy, and the fuzz are always looking over their own silly shoulders at their own silly legal advisors. They're scared of chaps in the Home Office, and scared of crusty old judges dozing away on their benches and in their chambers. So they go in for cunning inactivity a good deal.'

'What we need is cunning of an active order,' Lou said.

'Call it just action,' Dave said. 'Pile into the scrimmage, and without being too particular about dangerous use of the feet. Nobody's going to blow a whistle in this game.'

Averell didn't find Dave's image heartening. He dimly recalled mixed hockey as an extremely hazardous sport. Mixed rugger didn't bear thinking about. He wanted to say, 'But we're not on a playing-field, and the people we're after have twice attempted murder.' But he refrained, aware that any wet-blanket effect he put up would now be merely counter-productive. And this was the state of the case when they arrived at Uffington Street.

It proved to be in a distinguishably run-down area near Holland Park. The houses were enormous affairs that might have been described as 'towering' a generation ago, and they looked as if the same generation had passed since anything much had been done to their peeling stucco. The bank was tucked into the ground floor of one of them, and presented the only trim appearance in the row. Dave slowed down as they came abreast of it, and they took a good look at this first scene of action. Business was going on there as usual; there might be chaos and lurking squads of police within; customers, however, were coming and going with complete unconcern. Averell had been supposing, in his uninstructed manner, that the final assault upon its strong-rooms must have required the use of high explosive, and that there would be shattered windows (a sight familiar on television) all around. He even felt a shade of disappointment that this was not so. It wasn't a sensible feeling at all.

And now here was the squatters' house. Dave drew his car to a halt, and leapt out of it in a fashion suggesting the arrival of Action Man in the imagination of a rumbustious small boy. They all jumped out and, as it were, stormed the place. Anybody watching (and what sinister adversary, after all, mightn't be?) would have felt that something decisively dramatic was in hand. There was, in fact, one visible watcher in the person of a constable stationed on the pavement close to the front-door steps. The constable made no movement; he did, indeed, cast an eye on these arrivals, but it was with an air of indifference which, if tempered by anything at all, was tempered only by a mildly benevolent regard. The front door was ajar. They marched in.

There was a big shabby hall, floored with cracked tiles which had once been designed to simulate the splendours of marble paving in a bold and obscurely Pompeian design. It was unfurnished except for an abandoned receptacle in chipped porcelain which took the grotesque form of the severed leg of an out-size elephant. Incongruously, there were a couple of quite spruce umbrellas located in this, together with a short thick stick, bulbous at the end, which Averell thought of as a knobkerrie, and which might certainly have been accepted as an offensive weapon if produced before a magistrate. But, if Tim and his friends were right, squatters were invariably wholly inoffensive persons. Perhaps this object had been left around by some former tenant with an interest in African antiquities.

There was a sound of conversation – or rather of monologue – from one of the ground-floor rooms – the door of which Dave promptly opened to usher them all inside. It contained a large packing-case which served as a table, and round this was ranged a much over-stuffed three piece suite. On the sofa two small children of indeterminate sex were engaged in fisticuffs of a controlled and decorous sort. In one chair a mild-looking man with square spectacles and a square-cut beard was reading aloud in what Averell instantly recognized as the tongue of ancient Greece; he was being listened to by a woman suckling a baby in the other. The man put down his book at their entrance, and various introductions were performed. They might have been taking place in a drawing-room in one of the better parts of Kensington. But here were squatters, all the same. Nobody seemed to feel anything untoward in their situation. Averell, although he succeeded in producing conventional murmurs in proper form, was naturally a little at sea.

'Yes, indeed,' the bearded man (whose name was Adrian) was saying to Tim, 'we were closely interrogated about the whole affair. It was perfectly proper, no doubt. And we were accorded a civil congé in batches as soon at it became apparent that we were substantially without criminal proclivities. But some are still – I fear, and as the vulgar phrase has it – helping the police with their inquiries. All in all, it has been undeniably a vexatious episode.'

Tim failed to receive this temperate and cultivated speech too well. Presumably Adrian (and his wife and children, as they no doubt were) belonged to a section of squatting society of which he was unable wholly to approve. Yet they seemed likely to be less devoted to pop music than to Bach, and presented very much the domestic note which Tim had been anxious to capture for the edification of the readers of *En Vedette*. More muddle, Averell told himself. Adrian must belong to what he had somewhere seen described as the overqualified unemployed. Nobody would hire him to give public readings of Xenophon (for the book was in fact the *Anabasis*) and he was perhaps very reasonably disinclined to take up any less learned employment. Averell felt an immediate sympathy with this person, in whose shoes he himself might conceivably be standing but for the convenient fortune handed on to him by his father. It had to be admitted, however, that Adrian appeared to be a man unlikely to assist at all notably in the running to earth of a gang of crooks. (But this, as frequently with Averell's conjectures, was to prove not entirely accurate.)

'I think we ought to have some tea,' Adrian's wife announced in a pleasant but distinctly upper-class accent. She had satisfied the requirements of her infant and composedly returned him (or her) to a soap box which Averell had not previously noticed as an additional furnishing of the room. 'And I shall invite Twite,' the lady added. 'Twite is a little cast down because the police are still holding on to his wife. It seems that the poor dear – really the sweetest woman, Mr Averell – has quite a record of receiving stolen goods. Only in the way, it seems, of what are apparently called second-hand wardrobes. The term is a misleading one, and suggestive of discarded furniture. It means old clothes.'

'Mr and Mrs Twite,' Adrian said seriously, 'having cast off clothing of every description, cordially invite personal inspection. I can recall the admirable couple as advertising in a newsagent's window in those terms. One would suppose a jest or *équivoque* to have been intended, but they have assured me it was not so. By all means, Hortensia, bid the good fellow to a dish of tea.'

'That will be very nice,' Tim said – but not in the tone of one who believed that a quiet tea-drinking was at the moment the appropriate thing. 'But I'll just show Uncle Gilbert round while it's brewing.' He led Averell from the room. 'I know Twite,' he then said. 'A harmless little man, and it's a great shame they're holding on to his equally harmless little wife. I wonder whether I could get hold of a solicitor and make a row?'

'I don't at all know. Nor do I know, Tim, just where we're going. Whether we're after those people as bank robbers or as would-be murderers, I can't see what happens even if we run them to earth. You can't be imagining visiting some purely private retribution on them. The only possibility would be to call in the police.'

'Oh, yes – I suppose so. But at least we'd be showing the fuzz we can out-point them at their own game. They'd look uncommonly silly, wouldn't they, if we marched this whole gang in on them already in fetters? I wonder where one can buy fetters? There must be people who cater for eccentric tastes by selling manacles and whips and things.'

In face of this childishness Averell gave up again, and they began to wander through the house. Fewer of its former occupants had returned into residence than Tim had appeared to expect. Averell felt this to be scarcely surprising. The new race of beings to whom he was being introduced were of at least semi-nomadic habit, travelling so light that they could very readily move on to quarters less unpropitious than the Uffington Street house had proved to be. In one upstairs room there was a group of half a dozen young men and women in a state of torpor into which Tim seemed indisposed to inquire, and in another there was a family rather like Adrian's, except that its head was absorbed not in the *Anabasis* but in an outdated copy of the *News of the World*. There were also three elderly women who sat knitting in an empty room in a sinister and Norn-like manner. None of these people seemed much interested in the recent sensational events in the house.

'We'd better go down to that tea party,' Tim said, 'and then think again.' He appeared to be discouraged by the results of this exploration so far. 'These people are all half-witted, more or less. And I wonder about searching the place thoroughly? We might come on some sort of clue.'

'We might, Tim. But it isn't at all probable. I expect the police are at least pretty efficient at that.'

'They've sealed up both entrances to the cellars where the tunnel begins. So it's no go there. Hullo! What was that?'

Somebody had given a peremptory shout from the hall to which they were now descending. And this was immediately repeated on a yet louder note.

'Electric!' the voice bellowed. It proved to belong to a heavily moustached man, wearing dark glasses and carrying a clipboard and an electric torch. 'Never been here before,' the man said in an aggrieved manner. 'Where's the bloody meter?'

'Where you bloody find it,' Tim replied cheerfully. 'I don't carry it round with me, mate.'

The man gave an indignant snort (which was not wholly unjustifiable) and disappeared into a room on the right of the hall, which could just be glimpsed as probably constituting the sleeping quarters of Adrian and his family.

'How very odd,' Averell said. 'I'd expect the electricity and gas to be switched off when a house is being occupied in this – well, irregular manner.'

'The owner often leaves them on and foots the bill, as a matter of fact. Random means of heating and lighting and cooking is disliked by insurance companies as enormously increasing the risk of fire. Here he is again. He won't have had any luck in there.'

The electricity man had emerged and was making across the hall. He threw open the door of Adrian's living-room and marched in. Tim and his uncle followed. The occupants were already at tea, and had been joined by a diminutive man with an indecisive beard who was presumably Mr Twite.

'Where's your meter?' the intruder shouted again, and glared around him. Despite his glasses, it appeared to Averell possible to

166

detect that he was a good deal more inter-ested in the company than in the where-abouts of the elusive meter. And it was perhaps Dave who particularly arrested his attention. 'You,' he said aggressively. 'Do you know where it is?'

'Look in the cupboard at the back of the hall, you great oaf.' Dave was uncommonly angry. 'That's where the thing's usually found. And clear out. We don't like you.' Dave had got to his feet, and was advancing upon the intruder in a manner sufficiently hostile to send him hastily backing out of the room, banging the door behind him. There were several more bangs – the last of them as this outrageous person, having pre-sumably effected his purpose, left the house.

'Horrible chap.' Dave said, retrieving his teacup. 'No manners at all.'

'You were perhaps a little short with him yourself, Dave,' Adrian said mildly. Adrian, although pouring tea into cracked mugs with perfect propriety, could be detected as anxious to get back to Xenophon. 'But I must say that I was a little doubtful about him. Did anybody ask him for his card?'

'His card?' Dave repeated. 'You mean a visiting card?'

'Oh, no – not that.' Adrian was un-conscious of any ironical intention in Dave's query. 'I doubt whether persons of that sort ever carried anything of the kind. But I believe the electricity company, if that be the name for it, commonly provides its employees with the means of authenticating themselves. As it is, he might have been a criminal. And we don't want anybody of that kidney here.'

'Do you know,' Mr Twite said suddenly, 'that I believe I've seen him before? Or, rather, heard him before. Yes, I am confident I recognized the voice. Rather a nasty voice. Not that he wasn't a most satisfactory customer. Undiscriminating, perhaps. But decidedly free with his cash.'

'Just what do you mean by that?' Tim had straightened up alertly. 'In your shop, was it?'

'Yes, in my business premises.' Twite turned to Averell, whom he seemed disposed to treat as a person of superior consequence. Twite was another individual who had Averell guessing. He couldn't quite be called a cockney, but he certainly hadn't been Tim's or Dave's schoolfellow. 'We carry, I must explain, a very large stock, a very large stock indeed, and lately we have followed a policy of diversification. It's why we're no longer able to live above the shop, my wife and I. Upstairs is now part of the shop too.'

'So what?' Dave asked.

'This man – I'm sure it was this man, although he hadn't those glasses or just that sort of moustache – came in and bought quite a lot in the garments department. That, you know, was our original line, and we're very strong in it. He had rather a garish taste, running to what you might call the drop-out image in a rather heavy fashion. Male garments, you understand, and a good deal in the way of accessories. We're strong on accessories as well. Rather barbaric stuff, I'd say he chose. He explained, you see, that he was setting up four or five young friends in business as a pop group. Why, have I surprised you?'

The party from Boxes were certainly surprised; they were considerably startled as well. Here, out of the blue, was confirmation of pretty well the only theory of the robbery they had arrived at.

'And then he went up to the musical instruments,' Twite went on. 'That's rather a new departure with us, and we're not too knowledgeable about it, to tell you the truth. I never could remember, myself, which is a viola and which a violin. Not that he wanted obsolete affairs like that. Come to think of it, though, he did buy a double bass, complete with a case the size of a coffin. And half a dozen other things as well – and with no more than a casual twang at any of them before forking out the asking price. A most satisfactory customer, as I said.'

'I don't suppose,' Tim asked, 'that he had any notion that you and your wife had moved in here?'

'Of course he hadn't. How could he? We don't advertise the fact. Our image might suffer if we were thought to be in straitened circumstances.'

Anne and Lou, who had sat silent during the making of this remarkable communication, now both spoke at once – and to what proved to be the same effect. Why had this munificent patron of *avant-garde* music incontinently transformed himself into a reader of electric meters? No prize need be offered for the answer. It had been his business to confirm that Dave had not been satisfactorily warned off the trail by the message planted on him by the fat woman on the M4. So they'd better take care of Dave. Otherwise Dave might be taken care of in the sinister sense of the phrase current in the world of gangsterdom.

At this point Dave behaved much as if the sun were shining on him again. It was as if he hadn't really liked playing second fiddle to Tim as a threatened person, and was delighted by this evidence of having received promotion. But Dave's changed manner, Averell felt, was only to be accounted for in part on this assumption. It was as if some perception had come to him which he was disposed to keep to himself for the present.

'Well, well, well!' Dave said in his easiest manner. 'And did this admirable customer of yours leave his name and address, by any chance, and arrange for you to deliver the goods?'

'Dear me, no.' Twite seemed to regard this idea as absurd. 'Ours is a cash and carry business, you see. Our transactions are invariably on that footing. Transport is the customer's liability. We write that up, in fact, on a notice in the shop – along with "Please do not ask for credit. A refusal may offend". It's always as well to be clear about those things.'

'So what did the chap do?'

'He had a little tip-up truck, with a two-wheel light trailer hitched on behind it. He simply piled the stuff on that, paid up, and drove away.'

'A pity you didn't follow him,' Dave said.

'Why on earth should I follow him?' Twite was perplexed. 'His fivers were all right. I know a forged fiver by this time, believe you me.'

'Yes, of course. Well, there's no possibility of trailing the villain to his lair. So let's begin to think of another plan. Half a minute, though. I'm going to the loo.'

With this simple announcement, Dave left the room. Adrian's wife (who appeared to confine herself to domestic cares and the exercise of hospitality) watered the teapot. Adrian's children now sat at each end of the sofa, munching biscuits. Some little time elapsed. And then a sound from the street brought Anne to her feet and hurriedly to the window. It was the sound of a departing car. Anne turned round.

'That was Dave,' she said. 'He has just driven off – and without a word! What can it mean?'

'Dave's sometimes taken that way, Anne.' Tim, although clearly much troubled, said this quietly. 'He's not ditching us or anything. He'll be back.'

'I believe he tumbled to something we didn't,' Lou said. 'And he's off to take advantage of it. I call it a bit mean.'

'It's nothing of the sort – and we must just hope it isn't dangerous. Dave sees a thing, you see, and charges at it. Ever since a kid, he's had an urge to be the lone ranger.'

14

Several hours went by, and Dave didn't come back. Midnight arrived. There was no Dave still.

Nothing so uncomfortable had ever happened to Gilbert Averell before. The mere physical unease for a start irked him to an extent he'd have been ashamed to confess. The resources of Adrian's *ménage*, although made freely available, were limited in the extreme. When the children had been put to bed Averell was accommodated on the sofa, and the young people scrounged around and borrowed several kitchen chairs. At a late hour they all drank more tea and consumed an emergency supply of fish fingers. It was rather like being in a play by Samuel Beckett, wherein all things are reduced to an absolute minimum.

But much worse than this, of course, was the nervous strain of waiting for Dave. Oddly enough, the person who seemed to feel this most acutely was Adrian, who at one point became so fidgety that his wife was constrained to suggest a resumption of the reading from Xenophon. As she herself was obviously able to follow the language, as

Tim had 'done' Greek at school and could still understand bits and pieces now and then, as Averell was obliged to admit considerable classical accomplishment, and as Twite had departed, this left out only the two young women, and such was their desperation that they both stoutly declared that they would be happy to listen in. So this bizarre exercise was indulged in for the better part of an hour. But by that time the vanguard of the Ten Thousand had reached the summit of Thekes and were shouting so wildly that Xenophon was hurrying up from his pest of danger at the rear, expecting some disastrous ambush. Nothing of the kind. His soldiers had glimpsed the sea. *Thalassa, thalassa!* At this supreme moment in historiography Adrian broke down, and declared that he could no further go. The three other scholars present found this emotion infectious. Anne and Lou were mystified but impressed. They brewed yet more tea.

For Averell the one point of comfort in all this was the thought that his companions were at least realizing their helplessness. The villains might by now be chopping Dave into messes with a barbarity equalling Xenophon's Persians at the top of their form. Nothing could be done about it. Clue or lead as to Dave's intentions and where-abouts there was absolutely none. So a breaking-point must come, Averell thought, when they must all hurry off to a police station. Even so, they'd have a weird story that would take quite some time to sort out. And it was hard to see what the full might of the Metropolitan Police could effect, except to start a hunt for an elderly Bentley or a small tip-up truck with a trailer hitched behind it.

Of course this was to take the darkest of several possible views – as the young Xenophon had done when he heard all that shouting. It was conceivable that Dave was on top of the situation, always supposing that there was a situation to be on top of. He might simply be off on the most harmless, if futile, of wild goose chases. It was even possible to feel that the sober probabilities lay that way. But Averell found that he couldn't persuade himself of this for many minutes on end. He had the wild thought – almost the hopeful thought – that he had misjudged Dave's toughness; that the boy had lost his nerve and (as his companions might say) chickened out on the whole affair. Alternatively (and not quite so horribly) he might have driven his great car so furiously through London that a serious accident had resulted and Dave had been carried off in an ambulance.

'What about the hospitals?' Averell asked, breaking a long silence. 'Can one ring round the casualty wards and ask for information?'

'There must be scores of them,' Tim said shortly.

'Yes, of course. But don't you think that all information about serious accidents is centralized at once; that somewhere the police have an hour-by-hour record of the lot?'

'We must give it time. We must give Dave time,' Tim produced this doggedly and (Averell thought) almost pig-headedly. 'In the morning, yes. But now we'd better go to bed.'

'I believe that would be the judicious thing,' Adrian said this with an odd mingling of firmness and perturbation. 'There are one or two things that have to be thought out. I very much feel the need of that myself.'

'Adrian, whatever do you mean by that?' Tim demanded. 'If you have something to say, for Christ's sake say it.'

'No, no. In the morning, perhaps – as you say yourself.' Adrian stood up. 'We had better look around for sleeping quarters. Hortensia and I, that is. The girls must clearly have our bed.'

'Nothing of the sort,' Tim said, with a good deal of his old decisiveness returning to him. 'We can still get a taxi. Anne, can you take Lou home with you?'

'Yes, of course. I was given the prescriptive latch-key quite some time ago.'

'Good! And Uncle Gilbert can come back with me to the flat. There will still be nobody else there. And at least the beds weren't blown to bits. We'll rendezvous here at breakfast-time.'

This plan – whether prudent or not – was agreed to. By Averell it was because he welcomed an opportunity of a certain amount of private talk with Tim, and because it looked like getting the young women into security and decent accommodation at least for the remainder of the night. Tim went out to find a telephone kiosk and call a cab. His uncle insisted on going with him, on the principle that two might be better than one. What might be lurking around Uffington Street still one just couldn't tell. The effect was rather like that of the nocturnal prowl in the garden at Boxes. Only all that had harboured there had proved to be the absurd Gustave Flaubert. Here it might really be the people who had so definitely endeavoured to take care of Tim.

But the foray was uneventful, and the cab arrived. They dropped the girls at the kind of eminently respectable address that Averell had expected Anne to own. Then they went on to what Tim called his pad, where the effect was markedly different. Averell wondered whether Ruth and her daughters (by now fast asleep in Rome) so much as knew that the boy had a stake in what proved to be two floors of an almost derelict tenement building off the Mile End Road. But at least, as Tim had promised, there were beds, although Averell didn't yet feel he wanted to tumble into one. This wasn't because he didn't by now feel uncommonly tired. He did – and his nervous tone wasn't much improved by the still-evident havoc created by the letter-bomb. At least, however, this made it clear that Tim hadn't been imagining things. (By this time Averell was feeling a certain lack of confidence in everybody – a fact which was presently to appear.)

Tim was now for the first time his uncle's host in the full sense, and he acted properly in terms of solicitude for his comfort. This ran to the producing of a bottle of whisky from a cupboard stocked with drinks of various kinds. Tim poured a couple of not disturbingly lavish tots and signed for them on a scratch-pad provided for the purpose: a club-like arrangement which his uncle found reassuring. When they had sat down to this nightcap Averell cautiously asked a question.

'Do you happen to know, Tim, whether that odd chap Adrian and Dave have known one another for very long?'

'I don't know, but I rather imagine not. Why do you ask, Uncle Gilbert?'

'I felt that Adrian was even more disturbed

than the rest of us by Dave's failing to turn up again. It made me suppose that perhaps they are close friends.'

'I'm sure they're not that. But I did notice something myself. It was as if Adrian had something on his mind, but didn't quite like to come out with it.'

'Something like that, Tim. Might it have been because those girls were there?'

'I don't see why.'

'I got the impression that Adrian had never met them before, or at least that they were virtually strangers to him.'

'I see.'

'And I suppose there are things one doesn't talk about in the presence of girls – or not of girls one barely knows.'

'I hardly think there's much in that.' Tim buried his nose in his glass, and conceivably reflected on the familiar topic of the generation gap. 'Anyway,' he said presently, 'murder and bank robbery are perfectly respectable subjects. They're not of the *pas devant les domestiques et enfants* order, are they?'

'Now you're laughing at me.' The whisky was relaxing Averell a little. 'But about Dave himself, Tim. Are you sure he's a thoroughly reliable young man?'

'Reliable!' This time, Tim set down his glass and stared at his uncle. 'We were at school together. Schools, in fact, since we started at the same prepper. He's my oldest friend.'

'So he wouldn't rob banks.' Averell had no idea why he offered this absurd remark. 'Tell me a bit more about him. What does he do?'

'What does Dave *do?* He's like me – much too young for the world's work, Uncle Gilbert.' The whisky must have been affecting Tim too, since he was now being purely mischievous. 'Dave just drives about in that useless great thing – and is of course vastly concerned to improve the human condition.'

'Well, I'm sure that's very proper. But what are they going to *make* him do?'

'Oh, his father wants to put him into Lloyd's or the Stock Exchange or something equally shaming. Dave really does pretty well, if you ask me. He's under an enormous disadvantage, you know.'

'I'm very sorry to hear that.' Averell supposed it was to be revealed to him that Dave was an epileptic, or subject to bouts of religious mania.

'He's like me, as a matter of fact: an only son and with two sisters. But there the family resemblance stops. Poor old Dave has a father who's said to be the richest man in England.'

'And that's a kind of hereditary curse, would you say?' It wasn't clear to Averell why this interesting but scarcely startling piece of information had obscurely disturbed him.

'Well, yes. We make fun of him, of course, as an infant Croesus. But I suppose it's unfunny, really. If one happens not to believe that one should be able to write oneself out a cheque as big as twenty men's wages for twenty lifetimes, one is up against problems of family tradition and loyalty and all that. I'm damned glad I'm not in Dave's shoes.' Tim finished his whisky in sudden gloom; he was perhaps wondering whether this last remark mightn't represent an inadvertent dip into dramatic irony. 'And now we'd better get some sleep,' he said.

15

Getting sleep wasn't easy, at least for Gilbert Averell. He had been thinking of Dave – whose very surname he didn't know – as existing in a sort of social vacuum: a tough and independent young man, whose courses, even when hazardous, remained his own affair. But now Dave had suddenly been presented to him as possessing a father and sisters – and presumably he had a mother as well. To these people Dave's friends owed a duty which perhaps they hadn't got round to thinking of very clearly. If the young man hadn't turned up by the following morning, or at least managed to send a reassuring word about himself, his father at least ought to be let know. In fact for Averell, if he was to preserve any sense of himself as a responsible agent, there was now a deadline only a few hours ahead. All this private enterprise would have to be decisively wound up.

There was at least a relief in seeing this clearly. But before Averell did manage to fall asleep on it a further disturbing thought fleetingly visited him. He understood Tim's aversion to the police: it had a history behind it. And the two girls he felt as in a sense tagging along. Both Anne and Lou, indeed, had an air of independence, but essentially they did as Tim told them. Dave was in a different category, and about Dave he sensed (or thought he sensed) something elusive. He had found himself capable of some rather surprising conjectures about Dave. Tim in a final analysis (and if the term was not too derogatory) was something of a parlour anarchist. Dave mightn't be in the least like that.

These thoughts would have been very disturbing indeed had Averell not retained some sense that they were scarcely thoughts at all. They were a mere fooling around with figments, and if he went far with them he would find himself suspecting everyone of being capable of anything; of taking it for granted that nobody was what he appeared to be. And this state of mind (mildly paranoid, he supposed) was obscurely the consequence of the course of deception into which the accursed Georges had led him. It's a tangled web we weave when first we practise to deceive. With this tag in his head, Averell did finally go to sleep.

He slept heavily, and it was daylight when he woke up. There were voices in the flat. He scrambled out of bed (in his vest and underpants, which was an uncomfortable thing) and went into the bomb-blasted sitting-room. It was to find Tim talking to Adrian, who seemed just to have arrived – and in a condition that was making coherent communication difficult. Adrian, it seemed, had spent a very bad night indeed; he had got up early and walked all the way from Uffington Street; and now an exasperated and increasingly apprehensive Tim was trying to get some sense out of him.

'It was when Twite mentioned that double bass,' Adrian was saying. 'You remember that? It brought the thing back to me. But it seemed so unaccountable, so extremely upsetting, that I couldn't bring myself to speak up about it. It did, I mean, seem to require thought. But this morning I felt I must come and tell you at once.'

'Then for heaven's sake do!' It looked as if Tim would gladly have taken Adrian by the shoulders and shaken him. 'What about the bloody double bass?'

'I'll tell you. I'll tell you in a minute.' Adrian was now speaking quite wildly. 'But where's Dave?'

'What do you mean – where's Dave? It's what we all want to know, isn't it? Pull yourself together, man!'

'Isn't he here?' Adrian looked round the room in bewilderment, and for a moment stared at Averell as if he might be the missing young man in disguise. 'His car's here. Parked outside in the street.'

Simultaneously, Averell and Tim hurried to a window. And there, directly below them, the Bentley was.

'It's empty,' Tim said. 'And Dave certainly hasn't been here. Nobody has, except my uncle and myself. We'll go down and have a look. But first, Adrian, say what you have to say.'

'You remember what Twite said about the case?'

'The case! What case?'

'As big as a coffin. The case for the great big fiddle Twite said that man bought. I suddenly remembered I'd seen Dave with it. Or with its twin, of course. One couldn't be sure.'

'My dear Adrian,' Averell said, 'compose yourself.' Averell on his part wasn't feeling at all composed. 'Where was this, and when? Was it when one of those bands or groups or orchestras arrived in Uffington Street?'

'Not there at all. That would have been less queer, wouldn't it? I'd been to our public library. It's more than a mile off. And this van was outside some sort of empty shop next door to it.'

'This van – what sort of van?' Tim demanded. He had turned very pale.

'The tip-up van, I suppose. They were loading it with this and that. And Dave was shoving in that great big fiddle in its case. I think I only paid attention because he was pretty well staggering under it. But it was Dave, all right. What do you think it means?'

'It means that yesterday afternoon, when Twite was yattering, Dave remembered just what you're remembering now, Adrian. It means just that and no more than that.' Tim spoke grimly. 'So take a grip of yourself, Adrian.'

'But then Dave went off like that, and hasn't been seen since! He must have–'

'He must have taken it into his bloody thick skull to do another of his DIY acts.'

'DIY?' Averell said.

'Do It Yourself. Or Go It Alone. Now we'll go and look at the Bentley.'

Although without knowing precisely why, Averell had strongly disliked the look of the Bentley incongruously parked in this mean street. He was in considerable confusion of mind – so much so, indeed, that he forgot about the necessity of dressing himself and had to be packed off by Tim to huddle into his clothes. Adrian was now calmer; he had unburdened himself of his secret and had taken on the air of a hovering spectator, arrested by some inexplicable accident by the wayside but beginning to think of moving on and attending to his own affairs. He was a vague sort of man. Or he was this when not concentrating upon a Greek text.

There was a milk-float at the end of the street but otherwise it was deserted, and any

186

stir within-doors was still masked behind closed curtains and lowered blinds. The car was drawn up neatly by the kerb; the doors were unlocked; the key was in the ignition. They looked at it silently and fearfully for some seconds. Then Averell spoke.

'Tim, one simple explanation occurs to me. Dave may simply have left his car for you to pick up. Did he ever do that?'

'Never.'

'But perhaps,' Adrian said, 'he did it on this occasion, not wanting to disturb you in the small hours. There may be a message inside.'

'I don't think so.' Tim paused; he seemed reluctant to put this sanguine suggestion to the test. 'I think he discovered something – and it was important enough for him to drive here and tell my uncle and myself, bang in the small hours though it was. And then something happened. We don't know what. I'm wondering about touching those door handles. Because of fingerprints.'

'Very wise,' Averell said. He felt that Tim's mind had taken a propitious turn, since fingerprints were not of much use to a Robin Hood and his merry band. 'But perhaps you could use a handkerchief.' In periods of fatigue Averell occasionally read detective stories.

Tim used a handkerchief, and pulled open the front nearside door. It swung back silently. There was a faint smell of expensive leather upholstery mingled with a faint smell of tobacco smoke.

'No message,' Tim said. 'Nothing here. Except that there's something on the floor.' He put down a hand, and then drew it back quickly. 'Ugh!' he exclaimed, 'oil.' He looked at his hand, and so did Adrian and Averell.

'No,' Tim said slowly. 'Not oil. Blood.'

16

The shock of this discovery held them all silent for some moments. Then Tim spoke again in an unsteady voice.

'He'd discovered something, and he came to tell us. But they got ahead of him. They've had better luck with him than they had with me.'

'No, not that. Not if you mean they've killed him.' Averell heard himself speak with more conviction than he'd have supposed he could summon up in such a crisis. 'If they'd killed Dave they wouldn't have left his car on the spot for almost immediate discovery, while at the same time burdening themselves with his body. They'd have driven away the one in the other. So there must be a different explanation.'

'So there must.' Tim was now in command of himself again in a way that his uncle could only wonder at. Averell himself had seen – had just seen – death in war; Tim had never been tried that way. To Averell Dave was the acquaintance of a day, but he was Tim's oldest friend. If Tim could take this horror and remain instantly clear-headed Tim was a man, a grown man, one could rely on. 'And I'll tell you something,' Tim said. 'That fat woman and her clumsy threat. It was a stupid kind of temporizing. Behind it lay some sort of indecision. Dave was a potential threat. Just like me, he had only to remember something, to let something click in his head, and he'd become an actual one. But they'd come to see him as something else as well.'

'Do you know, I believe I may have an idea what it might be?' It was the learned Adrian who had said this, and still with the air of a detached spectator. He might have been a scholar who had just glimpsed some hope of resolving a minor but much debated textual crux in Sophocles or Aeschylus. 'Haven't I heard that Dave comes of rather wealthy people?'

'He does, indeed,' Tim said. 'I've been telling my uncle so. Enormously wealthy, as a matter of fact.'

'Then that's it. Those deplorable people have carried him off – and with a nasty scalp wound, as likely as not. But not for subsequent slaughter.'

'I believe you're right,' Averell said. Adrian too, he felt, had to be wondered at.

'They'd have two motives,' Adrian continued mildly. 'The bank robbery would appear to have been on a large scale, and they must require time to tidy up on it. To get the stuff away, I mean, and probably themselves away too. So – knowing he now *knew* – they'd want to hold on to him until that was effected. But alive, fortunately. And there's the second motive. Alive, Dave might be worth as much again. But it isn't so easy to collect ransom-money on dead bodies. Or not in the western world. There are, I believe, primitive societies in which a different view is taken. Even, indeed, in the Greece of the heroic age. To your uncle and yourself, Tim, I need scarcely cite instances in Homer.'

'No, you needn't,' Tim said grimly. 'What's important is to waste no time. And to keep this thing absolutely quiet for the moment.'

'To keep it quiet?' As Averell uttered these words he felt the return of a now familiar dismay.

'Yes, of course. When somebody has been kidnapped in the hope of monetary gain the one fatal thing is to hasten off to the police. Task forces go scurrying around, there are headlines in the papers, and it's even odds the criminals panic and chuck their victim into the sea or down a well. So we're on our own still.' Tim paused for a moment in which – momentously – Averell found nothing to say. This bee in his nephew's bonnet he had come to know there was no ready coping with. 'And listen!' Tim went on. 'There's one vital thing they don't know we know. They know what Dave remembered, and that it took him back yesterday evening to case their joint in that empty shop beside the public library. But they don't know that Adrian happened to witness that most extraordinary and mysterious occasion when Dave actually lent them a hand in loading up their van. My guess is that Dave just happened to be passing by and put on a turn in the way of gratuitous obligingness – the silly ass! And perhaps that gives us a tiny edge on them. So in we get.'

'But, Tim!' Averell did now manage to exclaim. 'We can't possibly–'

'Listen, Adrian.' Tim had ignored his uncle's expostulation. 'We'll run you back to Uffington Street and drop you there. You must cope with those two girls, but without giving them a clue about where my uncle and I are off to. We can't possibly have them mucking in on this thing as it's now developing. Lucky the bastards left the key in this bloody great car.' Tim was already at the wheel. 'Jump in,' he said.

They dropped Adrian off as proposed. He had provided vital information, and now for good measure a rational hypothesis covering the state of the case. But Tim clearly had no opinion of him as a likely man in a rough house. Uncle Gilbert, on the other hand, had been recruited at once. Uncle Gilbert (whom a punch on the nose had virtually worsted in the garden at Boxes) felt a very reasonable doubt about himself as a swingeing Friar Tuck. But Robin Hood had flattered him, at least by implication, and he went along. At least there were to be no Maid Marians involved, and that was something.

Tim seemed to know the location of Adrian's public library, and he parked circumspectly in a road behind it.

'When we find that shop,' he said, 'the best thing will probably be simply to walk in.'

'It may be locked up.' This was the only rejoinder Averell could think of to what seemed to him a staggering proposal.

'Then we bang on the door, and see what happens. If nothing does, we can bash our way through a window. It won't be the sort of shop with effective shutters of any kind. And if we just confront them in a perfectly confident way, the chances are they'll bolt in panic, leaving Dave behind them. It will be beyond their imagination that we haven't got the Commissioner of Metropolitan Police himself outside. You'll see.'

Averell judged it very improbable that he'd see – or hear or feel either, were this hair-raising psychological conjecture to be acted upon.

'But of course we'll be cautious,' Tim added, a little unexpectedly. 'We'll take a prowl round first, and particularly take a

look at the back. There may be a way in –
and out – at the back as well. Perhaps one of
us ought to go in at the back, and one at the
front.'

At this point Averell, had he been his
nephew's contemporary, might have said
something like 'Don't make me laugh' or
'You must be kidding'. As it was, he held his
peace. And he wondered whether it wasn't
unfortunate that Tim hadn't brought his
shotgun, or that he himself hadn't thought
to possess himself of that knobkerrie from
the elephant's leg at Uffington Street.

They took the cautious prowl, starting by
walking past the empty shop on the other
side of the road. It was a dirty and neglected
little property, which could just be distinguished as having once held itself out as the
place of business of a family butcher. This
was a little ominous in itself, but there was
no other sinister appearance to be seen.
They crossed the road to the public library,
where Tim insisted on pausing to study
some fading dust jackets displayed in a
window. As a move to allay the suspicions of
a possible observer this was unimpressive. It
had, indeed, the appearance of being a joke
– and a joke of an untimely sort, considering
Dave's possible situation at the moment.
Averell had to tell himself, not for the first
time, that his nephew wasn't in the least
mad; that the young in general weren't mad,

but merely variously inscrutable. Then they moved on, rounding a couple of corners in order to gain and identify the hypothetical back entrance to the failed butcher's establishment. This, in fact, brought them almost back to their parked car, and they were just short of it when the situation developed in a dramatic manner.

More or less under their noses a large decayed door swung inwards, and from a covered yard beyond it a vehicle propelled itself rapidly into the road and turned away from them. It was a tip-up truck. Two men could just be glimpsed in its cab. It was piled high with a load covered with a tarpaulin. In tow was a trailer, entirely occupied by a large crate, covered in part by a tarpaulin too. It disappeared in the direction of the main road.

'Quick!' Tim yelled, and made a dash for the Bentley. Averell followed – as he appeared perpetually destined to do. They bundled in; the engine sprang to life; Averell was bumped in the small of his back as the car accelerated at a tempo astonishing in so ancient and so lumbering-seeming a conveyance. It was quite as alarming, Averell thought, as being suddenly hurtled in the direction of the moon.

17

'It's our only chance,' Tim said as he slipped into top gear. 'Just not to let them out of our sight. Once they give us the slip we're done for. Not a hope.'

'They're bound to see we're following them. And they know this car already. At least we must suppose they do, after last night.'

'Well, yes – that's so. Provided they get a clear view of us. But it's quite possible they won't. With that affair in tow behind them, their rear vision must be about nil. The truck hasn't got one of those periscope things you use when hauling a caravan.' Tim slowed sharply, and then rapidly accelerated again. 'It's London that's going to be tricky. If we're held up by traffic lights and their route happens to branch off not far in front of them, we've pretty well had it. But once out in the country – if they're making that way – we needn't ever lose sight of them. And it won't much matter whether they tumble to us or not. We can hang on and be in at the kill, even if it's at Land's End or John o' Groats.'

Averell was silent – partly because one ought not to talk to the driver, and partly because he had judged Tim's figure of speech to be infelicitous. Of course if Dave were really where they both thought he was, his position, although it must be acutely uncomfortable, was far from being beyond hope of rescue. There need be no kill to be in at. His captors, if foiled in their ransom plot and virtually cornered, were unlikely to add gratuitous murder to their existing misdeeds. They'd simply try to bolt. Unless, of course, a live Dave knew far too much about them. And this – Averell realized with dismay – was about as big an 'unless' as one could conceive.

The truck wasn't hurrying, and its driver betrayed not the slightest sign of thinking to evade pursuit. With Holland Park behind it, it moved sedately down the length of Goldhawk Road, with its trailer swaying gently from side to side – and occasionally bumping rather drastically up and down – in the rear. It seemed improbable that any turn of speed could be extracted from it in however great an emergency. So in a sense it was an easy quarry.

'Remember how this road bears left?' Tim asked. 'If they go on to the end, and turn right for Chiswick High Road, it's my bet they'll be making for our old friend the M4. And I'm just wondering whether to take a chance – either here in town or out on the motorway.'

'A chance?'

'Well, yes. I wish they had Dave in a cage and not in that crate – if he is in that crate. The rub's there, wouldn't you say, Uncle Gilbert? If he were in a cage – like that king in *Tamburlaine* – he could gibber at us, and we'd know. But of course it might perturb the passersby.'

'Certainly it might.' Tim, his uncle supposed, was entertaining himself with this bizarre fantasy by way of what he would have expressed as keeping his cool. Averell himself found the notion of a young man pinioned in a crate so extremely horrible as to be an unsuitable subject for anything of the kind. But he saw the underlying cogency of Tim's line of thought.

'It would be easiest on the motorway,' Tim went on – swinging, as predicted, into Chiswick High Road. 'Just draw level with the thing, force it on to the soft shoulder, and then give it and ourselves a good immobilizing bash. There would be a crowd in a jiffy, including your friends the fuzz. But suppose that crate holds nothing but their swag – or even just a collection of miscellaneous musical instruments? If swag, we'd be heroes in the eyes of the bloody bank, of course. But it mightn't much improve Dave's chances if in fact they're holding him elsewhere.'

The lucidity of all this was apparent, and

Averell acquiesced in it. What disconcerted him now, oddly enough, was the gentle pace, almost the unflawed decorum, of this morning drive through the western outskirts of London. The occasional casual turning on of a television set a little before some desired programme was a habit that had familiarized him with the habitual climax of that sort of entertainment in which cops catch robbers. Salvos are exchanged, sirens ululate, cars squeal, skid, turn themselves incontinently into roundabouts. This was not like that, and so a naive expectation of drama was frustrated in him.

'That confounded thing might be a hearse,' he said testily – and was immediately appalled by the unfortunate implication of this remark.

'In which case,' Tim said grimly, 'it's our job to track it to the crematorium. But we'll hope it's not as bad as that. Yes! There's the flyover ahead. So it's as I thought. We'll be going west.'

Averell almost managed to find this echo of his own *phrase équivoque* (an expression his friend Georges would have admitted) tolerably funny, and he was further relaxed by the fact that their pace presently picked up considerably. If he wasn't exactly looking forward to a confrontation with the two toughs (as they must be) in the truck, he wasn't inclined to shirk it either. And if it were to be done at all (he told himself, vaguely recalling Macbeth) then 'twere well it were done quickly. He was almost disposed to urge his nephew to step on it and have his bash. On the motorway, which they had now gained, there was a great deal of traffic moving out of London, and the frenzied weaving in and out promoted by such situations would render at least the preliminary manoeuvring the more colourable.

But Tim was in no hurry, and his uncle had soon to conclude that he had abandoned the notion of a contrived collision. It was indeed true that if Dave wasn't in the crate, and these men were arrested on the discovery of stacks of banknotes, the move might eventually prove counter-productive so far as Dave's safety was concerned. And if Dave *was* in the crate even a small miscalculation (such as Tim's own car-driving assailant had committed) might not be at all healthy for him. Which all went to show that Tim was possessed of more native caution than some of his suggestions might lead one to expect.

'There's a panda car behind us,' Tim said suddenly.

'A what, Tim?' The expression was unfamiliar to the expatriate Averell.

'A police patrol car. It's been there for quite some time. Could it be of any use to us? I think not. We could wave it down and report. But the end-position mightn't be improved much by their bringing those chaps in. Not if Dave isn't there.'

'I'm not sure that I agree.'

'Can it be trailing us, do you think?' Tim had ignored his uncle's remark. 'Don't I look like somebody who drives a Bentley? At least I own a driving-licence, although I haven't got it on me. What about you, Uncle Gilbert? Could you prove yourself to be somebody respectable?'

All that Gilbert Averell could prove himself to be (it was an astonishing fact) was the Prince de Silistrie. That passport was still in his pocket, and so was a considerable sum in francs, along with a little small change in English currency. The sudden minor alarm occasioned by this reflection was merely ludicrous. It disturbed Averell, nevertheless.

They were in the middle lane, and now the police car in the fast lane drew level and slowed beside them. It contained two policemen, who studied Tim and his uncle with some curiosity. This seemed quite gratuitous behaviour, and as such was discomposing. The panda car, however, then moved on, switched with due notice to the middle lane, and similarly paused abreast of the truck, which was in the slow one. The truck seemed to interest them even more. Perhaps they were judging it to be injudiciously loaded, or perhaps there was something irregular in the way the trailer was hitched to it. But again there was anticlimax. The police returned to the fast lane and rapidly diminished ahead of them.

'Good riddance,' Tim said comfortably. Then he glanced into his driving mirror and added, 'Well, I'm blessed!'

'What is it this time, Tim?'

'Another one. Two more, in fact. There they go.'

And there, certainly, they had gone. Two further police cars had swept past them at speed.

'Going to a football match, I expect,' Tim said. 'Or to look after some minor royals at Windsor. There it is. See Windsor's domes and pompous turrets rise. Pope doesn't mean "domes", Uncle Gilbert. He just means "halls", or something like that. Latin *domus*, you see.'

'No doubt.' Averell took this burst of pedantry (Oxford pedantry) on his nephew's part to indicate rising spirits. Averell's own spirits were not quite managing that. It was with a certain wistfulness that he had seen all those policemen vanish into distance.

'And "pompous",' he said with an effort, 'means "characterized by stately show".'

'Alpha, Uncle.' Tim gave Averell a quick sideways grin before fixing his eyes on the road again. He was trying to keep three or four vehicles between the Bentley and the truck. 'But to business once more. When they quit the motorway and we're clear of all this traffic, they may possibly become aware of us, although I think it unlikely. Just in case, let's plan to seem to lose them without really doing so. Any ideas about that?'

'Well, yes – if their destination's right.' Averell had been thinking about this. 'They may just be making for another empty shop, or a yard or warehouse in an urban street. Slough, for example. If they did a sudden pull up like that, it wouldn't be much good just driving on and pretending not to notice. But if their next hide-out is a secluded place in the country – which seems probable enough – it might be managed that way. If they made a quick turn down a private drive, for instance, where the road was twisting and turning a bit, it might be possible to go haring past as if we thought they were still ahead of us.'

'In that case, so far so good, Uncle Gilbert. Aren't you a dab hand at this? But it wouldn't give them more than what might be called a breathing-space to rely on. Just comfortable time, come to think of it, for them to arrange a little reception committee if we did turn up.'

This lucid contribution to the argument was not encouraging, yet Tim himself seemed far from downhearted. He remained silent and thoughtful, however, over the next half-dozen miles.

'We must just rely on rapid improvisation when the time comes,' he said. 'Quick wits will be the order of the day. Do you think you and I are cleverer than they are? Top crooks are clever, of course. Everyone knows that. Much cleverer than the police, certainly.'

'Even than the top police?' Averell almost contrived to be amused at the unmistakable sound of the bees buzzing yet again in Tim's bonnet – or inside his head.

'Oh, yes – them too. You should read the books they write when they retire.'

'That's rather a different activity.'

'And it's why the fuzz use some act of parliament or other to clamp down on the record of their own efforts. But you and I *are* fairly smart, you know. I'm going to scrape a First in Schools if I ever go back to that dump.' (By this Tim presumably meant the University of Oxford.) 'And at Cambridge you came right at the top of your Tripos, I don't doubt.' Tim grinned again at his uncle, well aware that he was talking cock-sure nonsense. 'Hold hard!' he suddenly shouted. 'Action stations, Major Averell!' This seemed to be a whimsical reference to his uncle's long-past military career – the thought of which Tim always contrived to find amusing. 'They're going off.'

This was the first incontestably true remark that Tim had offered for some time. There was a junction ahead, and the truck was bearing left on the line of arrows leading to it.

'And we're in luck,' Tim said. 'Not Slough or Reading or any such ghastly place. Open country, winding lanes, and gents' secluded residences dotted around. Top crooks go in for your secluded residences – when it isn't phoney farms or derelict air strips. Let's hope they haven't a date with a private plane or helicopter. Proper Charlies we'll look if it's that.'

'There is a helicopter,' Averell said, and pointed upwards. 'I'm not sure it isn't hovering, just as if it's going to land.'

'Courage!' Tim commanded. 'The air's thick with such things round about here. We're still not all that distance from Heathrow. Don't say you're wishing you were back there and bound for Paris, Uncle Gilbert.'

'These scoundrels may be wishing they were just that.'

'Brazil or Guatemala, more likely, in their case.'

There was now only an empty road between themselves and the truck, and the truck was in fact out of sight beyond a bend. During all this chat the scene around them had changed entirely – and much as Tim had predicted. The road meandered, and off it on either side mere country lanes meandered too. There was even the roof-top of what Tim declared to be veritably a secluded gent's residence visible on their left.

'Aha!' Tim cried suddenly. The truck was in sight again, but only momentarily. It had swung abruptly off the road and vanished. 'This is where we drive on like mad,' Tim said. 'With one or two loud toots if the corners at all justify them.' Taken by this idea, he tooted now – rejoicing, his uncle supposed, in the possession of a guile unknown to the dull minds of the constabulary. They drove on in this way for something over half a mile, and then Tim drew the Bentley abruptly to a halt on a convenient grass verge. 'So here we are. Button up that combat-jacket, Major. Foot-slogging now. And we turn into Red Indians later on.' They scrambled from the car, and Tim locked its doors with a promptitude that would have done credit to a well-trained constable. 'What we shall have to think up pretty quick,' he said, 'is something in the way of diversionary tactics. Avanti, Uncle Gilbert! The curtain rises.'

18

And red Indians they did become. It wasn't a ploy that Averell could have imagined himself as much relishing had he been drawn into it by, say, a band of nephews and nieces much younger than Tim. He was without any impulse (such as uncles ought to have) to join in the imaginative games of children on call. Not many years before, had Tim, Kate and Gillian so summoned him, he would have produced some good-natured excuse, relapsed into his book, and assuaged a subsequent sense of guilt and insufficiency by tipping them all with unusual liberality at their next parting. But on the present occasion he was no sooner down on his belly than he was taking satisfaction in the thought that although an elderly, he was by no means an out-of-condition man. It was a reasonably flat belly, and the muscles controlling this unwonted mode of progress responded surprisingly well. And his eyesight was good. If that possibly fatal dry twig lay in his path he wasn't going to fail to spot it in time.

'Over to the right a bit,' he heard himself direct Tim in a most approved whisper. 'So that we'll still be under cover of those 'bushes ahead.'

Tim crawled to the right at once, and his uncle fleetingly recorded to himself once more the curious fact that his nephew, who habitually bossed him around, in fact took an order from him the moment it was given. There was a kind of weight of responsibility in this. He mustn't in a crisis – and wasn't there certainly going to be a crisis? – say the wrong thing.

Rather as if covert behaviour were infectious, the house seemed to be crouching behind hedges and shrubberies too. At one point in their cautious approach it even disappeared entirely, leaving them disoriented in a small forest of rhododendrons. Averell disliked rhododendrons, particularly when prematurely heralding the spring with a tasteless exuberance of conflicting hues. And beneath rhododendrons, moreover, the going is always for some reason so particularly dusty as to be distasteful to even the most intrepid brave. Quite suddenly, however, this garish barrier gave out, and the house was uncomfortably close in front of them – seeming to glare at them, indeed, from a score of upper windows like malignant eyes. It wasn't to be supposed that, in their present situation, Averell and his nephew would fall in love with the place at sight; but it seemed equally certain that no reasonable being could greatly care for it

even under the most favourable circumstances. It was a hypertrophied not-quite-
modern villa, all gables and bogus timbering
and ill-proportioned fenestration, and it was
neither on the one hand deservedly derelict
and in disrepair nor on the other decently
cared for in any evident way. Perhaps it was
just right as a temporary hide-out for male-
factors conducting business on a generous
scale. In front of it lay what appeared to have
been at one time a broad lawn, but this had
been converted in a rough-and-ready
fashion into a large gravelled and now ill-
weeded sweep on which one felt that large
cars could circle in an impressive fashion.
But the weeds would not, of course, have
afforded cover to a mouse – or at least not to
a stray cat – and this made further direct
progress impracticable.

'We'll try the back,' Tim whispered. 'It's
my bet the dump will break down into a
tumble of useless outbuildings that nobody
goes near any longer. Unless you feel it
would be better simply to march up to the
front door and ring the bell.'

Averell didn't feel this at all, and they
resumed their painful progress on a wide
arc. When this was achieved Tim proved to
have been right. The back of the house
presented two abandoned wings straggling
out in offices of diminishing consequence,
and the fourth side of a large concreted area

between them was closed by a large free-standing structure which seemed to hover in character between a warehouse and a barn.

'The bloody van!' Tim breathed. 'With its trailer still. But where's the crate? Gone!'

This was indeed the state of the case. The tip-up was parked before what must be the main back-entrance to the house, with its tarpaulin-covered load still piled up on it. But on the trailer there was nothing but its own tarpaulin, roughly folded and with a coil of rope beside it. It was – there could be no doubt of this – a spectacle of an indefinably sinister sort.

'Freeze!' Tim whispered.

This was an unnecessary injunction, since Averell was already very effectively frozen. Two men had emerged from the house and were climbing back into the cab of the truck. The truck then moved slowly across the yard and halted before the door of the barn-like building opposite. Simultaneously this was opened from within and two more men appeared. All four proceeded to strip the truck of its tarpaulin, unload its contents, and carry them into the interior of the barn.

As this operation was certainly of an illicit character one might have expected it to be carried out in a hasty and wary fashion amid evidence of guilt and unease. Nothing of the sort was evident. The four men worked with that sense of the worth of their own labour, and the moderate pace congruous with its dignity, which constitute (it may be thought) the true secret of England's greatness. It was Averell who felt guilty. Never before in his recollection – or never since the innocent pastimes of childhood – had he acted the part of a spy, or of any sort of vulgar peeper through chinks and crevices. And now he was doing so in immediate physical circumstances of particular indignity, since he and Tim had wormed their way within a small rectangular enclosure of crumbling brick which might at one time have served to accommodate a favourite pig, promoted to the status of domestic pet and as a consequence brought virtually within the curtilage of its proprietor's dwelling.

And might not this situation, so demeaning to two persons of some standing in the learned and academic world (for wasn't Tim, after all, going to take the same sort of distinguished degree as he himself had done?), be the result of some gross error or misconception about the whole affair? Trucks such as the one now under their surveillance were common enough; it was not unknown for them to trail subsidiary conveyances behind them; and it was impossible to be quite certain that the present outfit had emerged from what was indeed the back premises of that abandoned butcher's shop.

Some unfortunate coincidence might have bedevilled their whole design.

These implausible misgivings, although perhaps the issue of wishful thinking, received some support from the totally innocent appearance of what was going on. One of the men under observation was whistling as he worked; another had paused to light and enjoy a cigarette; the remaining two were exchanging uncultivated but good humoured badinage as they passed one another in the course of their task. What was being unloaded so far was a number of cardboard cartons of identical size and seemingly no more than moderate weight; they might contain, say, packets of breakfast cereal or rolls of lavatory paper or some equally innocuous variety of merchandise.

Averell was about to communicate these disturbing dubieties to his nephew when he was arrested by a change in the character of the freight being dealt with. The cardboard boxes had all been carried inside, and the men were now unloading what appeared to be a large number of small but heavy blue canvas sacks. These struck with Averell what was for some moments only a vaguely familiar note. Tim, however, clarified the situation at once.

'That's the hard cash,' Tim whispered with satisfaction. 'They cleared out the copper as well as the silver, if you ask me. Quite a wholesale job.'

Averell was constrained to agree at once. These were, of course, just the sort of bags that one observes being humped in and out of banks by the beefy and helmeted and leather-clad men who man the vehicles of security firms. So it was no longer possible to place even a remotely innocent construction upon the spectacle now being afforded. The barn-like building in front of them was nothing less than the repository of the ill-gotten gains of atrocious criminals.

The unfortunate Dave, however, was another matter. If he had indeed – as now seemed too likely – been conveyed to this remote hide-out in circumstances of horrible discomfort, if not remorselessly inflicted agony, he had been judged worthy of the enhanced security of the house itself. And there could be no doubt why he was here at all. If he were simply (as Tim had been) in the position of knowing too much it was certain that he would simply have been promptly taken care of (as Tim himself, if abortively, had been). The gang had arrived at a realization that Dave, alive, was probably worth much more than the total spoil to be obtained from a not particularly distinguished branch of a trading bank. The gang, in fact, had moved promptly into an alternative line of business.

Averell now saw that – lurking as he was in

this disgusting pigsty – an enormous responsibility had devolved upon him. He knew that Tim, so commanding and so given to hair-raising action, would, at a pinch, do as he was told by a senior man. (Public-school boys are brought up that way.) He himself had only to refrain from making suggestions and offering advice (which would be ignored) and, as it were, save up for the moment when an order must be given, and the thing would be on his own shoulders and not on his nephew's.

So what was the position?

It was much more hopeful than it might have been. Here was a cardinal fact. The story that Dave's father was the richest man in England was probably a picturesque exaggeration. Nobody in the world knows who is the richest man in England, although probably quite a number of people idly speculate from time to time as to whether they themselves fill the bill. But if one merely postulated great wealth in Dave's family it was almost a certainty that the family would pay up quietly whatever feasible ransom was demanded rather than risk the sort of battle of wits with the kidnappers that the police would probably favour. But would they? Averell, as if a little infected by his nephew's views on the fuzz, reflected that they mightn't be all that keen on setting the sort of trap that risks ending in failure and a panic killing. A quiet deal was perhaps something that they wouldn't, at least, very vigorously clamp down on.

So the broad facts of the case were simple. Dave's life was in no present danger. So far as the bank robbery went, he was no longer any sort of threat to the robbers, since he was their prisoner and would remain so until they had effectively covered up their tracks for good. And the ransom project was something to which they could then turn their attention at leisure. A period of silence after a kidnapping of this sort was even – Averell appeared to recall – a standard softening-up technique.

Of course the validity of this line of thought depended a good deal on Tim's confident assumption that the men with the truck had remained unaware of being followed; or that, failing this, they believed themselves to have successfully shaken off pursuit before the end of their journey. Were the criminals to conclude that their head-quarters had been discovered by adversaries still at large the entire situation would change at once.

At this point Averell's reflections were interrupted by an episode of minor drama. The truck had now been almost entirely emptied, but for some moments two of the men appeared to be struggling with a single remaining object of a bulky and awkward sort. They edged it to the ground with difficulty, and then with greater difficulty heaved it up between them and staggered with it into the barn. It was the case in which there ought to have reposed that Jumbo-sized musical instrument, a double-bass.

'What made the penny drop,' Tim whispered.

'The penny?'

'Inside Dave's thick skull. Even Dave knows that a big fiddle oughtn't to weigh a ton, since it's no more than a few slivers of wood wrapped round vacancy. Of course they used it to smuggle in their heaviest gear – and the stuff's in it now. Probably they had other bits and pieces in other cases, for bassoons and trombones and what have you. Cunning notion, smuggling themselves in as a band... Look, they're calling it a day.'

This was evidently so. The four men had emerged from the barn, and one of them was locking its door behind them. Then, leaving the truck where it stood, they walked across the yard and disappeared into the house.

'Come behind this wall,' Tim said, 'and we can at least stand up. How are you feeling, Uncle Gilbert?'

'Rather like the Empress of Blandings, I'd say.' Averell, whose reply had been prompted by a distinct impression that a faint porcine odour lingering in the sty had actually transferred itself to his person, wondered whether

216

this literary allusion remained intelligible to one of Tim's generation. 'Or,' he added, 'like Sancho Panza tagging after Don Quixote. So where's your next windmill, Tim?'

This was perhaps rather a testy joke, and inappropriate in the grim situation confronting them. Tim, however, took it in good part. Now behind the shelter of what might have once been a coal shed, he was helpfully dusting his uncle down with a flapping handkerchief.

'The house itself, I'd suppose,' he said. 'That's almost certainly where Dave is, so it's from there that we have to rescue him. But let's case that other building first. We're unlikely to get into the part they've stacked up their loot in, I suppose. But there may be more accessible bits and pieces at the back. I'd like to have a look – do a bit of a recce, as you used to say in your army days. Do you mind? I've rather an idea about the place, as a matter of fact. There may be ammo in it. Red Indians always have to steal their ammo, being poor ignorant bastards without the know-how to manufacture it.'

'Let's have a look, by all means.' Averell had felt something ominous about these remarks, having discovered by now that talking nonsense was often with Tim a prelude to outrageous action. But the 'recce' was at least preferable to an ill-advised march upon the house itself – which was certainly something that his nephew was perfectly capable of.

'Then here goes, Uncle Gilbert. And I don't think we need do any more crawling at the moment – do you? We just have to keep on the outer side of all these buildings to be safe enough. At least from bipeds, but of course one doesn't know about dogs. Wouldn't you expect these sort of people to go in for guard dogs? Alsatians and Airedales and Doberman Pinschers and Rottweilers. I don't think I've met a Rottweiler. They're said to be quite horrific.'

'Stop being an idiot, Tim.'

'Sorry.' Tim was now walking confidently ahead. 'But just keep your ears open for low growlings. You haven't heard anything of the sort, so far?'

'No, I have not.'

'Perhaps the dogs sleep by day, and just come on duty at night. But I'd rather expect a day shift as well as a night watch. Let's hope the no-dog effect isn't sinister.' Tim's excitement was mounting, so that his uncle wondered what in God's (or the Devil's) name he was cooking up. 'There's something like that somewhere in Sherlock Holmes. "Precisely, Watson. The significant point is that the hound didn't howl." It's something like that. The Hound of the Baskervilles had taken time off, and was simply basking in the sun.'

'Tim, for heaven's sake–'

'Don't look now, Uncle Gilbert.' Tim had halted dramatically. 'Or, rather, do. Take a good look, and tell me I'm not wrong. We've come bang on the kennels.'

This, like most of Tim's simply factual statements, was true. They had rounded another outbuilding, just short of the larger barn-like structure that was their goal, and had come upon a railed-in enclosure big enough to be rather suggestive of a prison yard or even a concentration camp. But what it seemed actually designed to accommodate was a pack of hounds adequate to the purposes of some eminently respectable Hunt – say the Craven Farmers or the Old Berks. From it there came no sound. But there did come a doggy smell. It was much more pronounced than the piggy smell that had hung around their late lurking place.

They stood contemplating this appearance more warily than would normally have been appropriate before a spectacle witnessing to the continued vitality of the most harmless (except to foxes) of English rural pursuits.

'I think I *do* hear something,' Averell murmured. 'But it's not exactly a low growling. And I'm not sure that fox-hounds go in for anything of the sort.'

'Then we'll take a look.' Tim walked boldly forward, and peered through the bars. 'March breast forward, Uncle Gilbert,' he said. 'What we've arrived at is the Seven Sleepers' Den.'

19

There were only three sleepers, and they certainly were not Christian youths of Ephesus, miraculously slumbering through two centuries of persecution. Tim, in fact, had spoken with decided poetic licence. And it wasn't even fox-hounds that were on view. It was three enormous dogs of anomalous breed. They lay stretched out on the concrete with their eyes closed and their tongues lolling from slavering mouths. One of them was snoring in a fashion so entirely human as to suggest that Circe had been at work on some sexually unsatisfactory wanderer. The others were breathing stertorously but without any appearance of discomfort. It was a surprising but not particularly alarming spectacle.

'I'd say they'd been drugged,' Tim said prosaically. 'What do you make of that?'

'That it's rather convenient from our own point of view. But Holmes may be right.'

'Holmes?' It seemed that Tim's recent chatter had gone out of his head.

'That the creatures' silence – or near silence – is significant. They're meant to kick up a hullabaloo if strangers come around the place. But that, just at present, wouldn't suit somebody's book. With dirty work going on, the gang is being careful not to alarm or alert the neighbourhood.'

'Uncle Gilbert, didn't I tell you that you have a genius for this sort of thing? *Nil desperandum Teucro duce et auspice Teucro.* Did I ever confess that I know you paid for my classical education? Thank you very much. And I hail you as Teucer now.'

'Teucer was an uncommonly good archer, and an enemy fell dead at every twang of his bow. So that cap doesn't fit. And it isn't recorded that he had to listen to a great deal of nonsense.'

'Then listen, Uncle Gilbert, and I'll say something reasonably sensible. There's a flaw in your theory about those somnolent dogs. They'd be unlikely to alarm the neighbourhood, because there simply isn't one. That was quite clear in the final stages of our getting here. As gents' residences in these parts go, this is a remarkably isolated one. That was no doubt part of its attraction for our friends.'

'True enough, Tim. Still, if those dogs have really been doped, it must have been to prevent their attacking or alarming *somebody*.'

'Not attacking. They were securely behind bars already – unless they were first drugged and then dragged and dumped here. But alarming, yes. It's a puzzle.'

'Perhaps it's possible–' Averell paused, since the idea in his head was so elusive that he had to grope for it. 'We keep on talking about the gang. Is it conceivable that there are two gangs?'

'I think I'd call one enough.'

'Yes – but one does read of such things. Gang warfare. One gang preying on another. There may be a rival gang, which has got wind of all that bank loot. It's preparing to take this place by assault now, and it has begun by silencing those dogs.'

'I think that's a bit far-fetched, Uncle Gilbert.' Tim said this with some severity, as if all extravagance of fancy was uncongenial to him. Then he frowned, and looked at Averell doubtfully for a moment. 'But do you know? It would fit in with rather a queer feeling I've been having from time to time since we arrived here. It's as if I had some sixth sense telling me we are under observation – and not from inside but from outside, so to speak. And I don't usually go in for rum feelings.'

'I'd suppose not.' Averell was in fact considerably startled by the suggestion of some dubious paranormal faculty lurking in his nephew.

'But of course there are perfectly adequate scientific explanations of such seemingly untoward phenomena.' Tim seemed to detect his uncle's discomposure, and to feel that it might be assuaged by a short expository lecture. 'What is in question is no more than a hyperacuity of one or another of the ordinary senses, the report of which presents itself only obscurely and at some rather elusive level of the mind.'

'I see. But now—'

'Quite often, though, the faculty operates at a fully conscious level. Shelley could distinguish the individual leaves of a tree at a range of a couple of hundred yards – and he thought nothing of it.'

'Tim, if we're being spied on, we'd better do something about it.'

'Well, at least do something about something.' Tim's untimely sense of mischief was in full play. 'In fact, just carry on. We're going to case that barn. Their strong room or treasury, one may call it. But the whole building can't be occupied that way. I've an idea that, here at the back, it may run to motor-sheds and store-rooms and so on with independent entrances. I know it doesn't sound interesting. But you never know what you may find. It mayn't be quite deserted, even. There may be a stray gangster around whom we can surprise and overpower and fiendishly torture until he renders up all the secrets of the conspirators. Are you a sadist, Uncle Gilbert? Did you enjoy tormenting the younger kids at that Belsen of a nine-

224

teenth-century public school?'

'For heaven's sake, Tim! It wasn't a Belsen, and it wasn't in the nineteenth century either.'

'That's no answer. I've often thought I'm probably a sadist. Now we'll see. Come on.'

Mercifully, no potential victim of these flesh-creeping fantasies was found. The barn itself was a brick and timber affair, and much too stoutly built to be broken into in a hurry. But at ground level several small chambers had been scooped out of it, and enlarged by wooden structures forming miniature wings. These were all unsecured. Two of them sheltered powerful cars, but the cars themselves were locked up. A third was a kind of store and small workshop, piled with the miscellaneous litter that accumulates in such a region of a big country house. Tim poked around it appreciatively.

'There's a jolly nice motor-mower,' he said when he emerged. 'The sort you sit on and whizz around like mad. But nobody seems to bother to use it, do they? Plenty of ammo, too.' He paused on this obscure remark. 'I wonder about that back door of the house itself. Could one use the mower as a battering-ram and bash it down? Then one could go roaring through the place, knocking the brutes down like nine-pins. It's an enticing thought.'

'It's very great rubbish, Tim.'

'So it is. I think the front door will be better. We'll go back there. Come on.'

Averell had by now been enjoined quite frequently to come on. And as on this occasion Tim didn't pause for compliance there was nothing for it but to follow him. To leave him unsupported was inconceivable, and it wasn't practicable to knock him down and tie him up until the orthodox forces of the law could be summoned at last. The real moment of crisis had come.

This time they rounded the house almost at the double, so that it seemed only moments before the front door faced them. It lay within an incongruous little classical portico, which was gained by a short flight of steps. Tim bounded up them, and his uncle followed. Here they were at least sheltered from any casual view.

'We ring the bell,' Tim said. 'We do exactly as I said we'd do at the butcher's shop.'

Tanto in discrimine, Averell told himself, as if succumbing to his nephew's recent penchant for Latinity. Here was the crunch. He nerved himself.

'No, Tim. We do nothing of the kind.'

'It will be perfectly all right. They'll be scared stiff, and simply cave in. We'll be negotiating on our own terms.' Tim put his hand out to the bell.

'No.'

'No?'

'Quite definitely not. We'd simply be handing them three hostages instead of one. I veto it.'

'Teucer speaking?'

'Teucer.'

'Then back to headquarters. Napoleonic change of plan.'

With these absurd words Tim turned and walked down the steps. This time at a dignified pace they both traversed the full length of the house and retraced their steps to the back. All those dozens of windows looked down on the conclusion of this amazing episode. It seemed incredible that they were not observed and pursued. Had they run as fast as they could on this abrupt retreat from Moscow the chances of detection would scarcely have been appreciably minimized. And it wouldn't, of course, have been good for morale.

The yard was as deserted as before. The truck still stood innocently in front of the barn. They took their former route to the back – Averell at least every moment expecting uproar and enraged pursuit behind them. But there wasn't a sound – or none except the heavy respirations of the stupefied dogs. Tim sat down on a bench, as if at the end of an afternoon's stroll through scenes of rural calm. He produced a packet of cigarettes.

'Have one of these?' he asked. 'Or what

about the pipe?' Averell made no reply, but sat down too. He had obviated, he felt sure, immediate disaster. But he had no idea of where they went next. Tim took a cigarette from the packet, tapped it in an old-fashioned way on a thumbnail, and struck the match. The match promptly went out.

'Have to dodge inside,' he said. 'Back in a minute.'

His uncle watched him disappear into the store-room. He must have been continuing to have difficulty in lighting up, because nearly a couple of minutes went by. Averell became conscious of a faint smell. It wasn't a doggy smell, nor was it the piggy smell from his own soiled garments. It was, in fact, the smell of petrol vapour. Then Tim appeared again. And suddenly behind him there was a back-cloth of leaping, of roaring flame.

'Better move away a little,' Tim said calmly. 'I'm afraid I was a little careless with that match.' He grinned happily as he glimpsed the appalled expression on his uncle's face. 'Ammo doing us proud,' he said. 'If we just had that double-bass we could play Nero to it, couldn't we? But of course we have other work on hand this afternoon.' He flung away his cigarette with the air of a conjuror dispensing with his wand. 'Action stations, Uncle Gilbert! The last battle begins.'

20

Had Timothy Barcroft begun at this point to execute a wild dance before the large-scale arson he had so effortlessly achieved his uncle would scarcely have felt surprised. But this would have been unjust to his nephew, who was no more a potential fire-bug than he was a thwarted sadist. Not that he wasn't taking satisfaction in the rapid progress of the conflagration he had occasioned. But this arose primarily (as was soon clear) from his conviction that he had achieved a tactical master-stroke, and perhaps in some sub-sidiary degree on the score of what might be called socio-economic theory: the per-suasion, to wit, that what was presently to be consumed to ashes in the barn was a mass of worthless paper purporting to be wealth in an acquisitive society. Robbers had been robbed in Uffington Street, and now the Uffington Street robbers were being robbed in their turn in a splendidly ironic manner. There was a kind of quiet bonus, as it were, of high-minded satisfaction in the contem-plation of this fiery spectacle.

'Softly, softly!' Tim was murmuring – apparently to the flames. 'Just go easy there.

We don't want our friends to have a lost cause on their hands too soon. And here they come, I think. Stir your stumps, Lord Emsworth. Back to the ghostly Empress.' Having thus signalled that he *did* know his P G Wodehouse, Tim took his uncle by the arm and conducted him at the double to the abandoned sty. It provided a flanking view of the ensuing proceedings.

The fire was already making a surprising amount of noise, and it was this that first alerted the unknown number of the enemy within the house. The back door had been flung open amid much shouting, and half a dozen men poured out into the yard. For a moment they stood halted in a bemused clump, as if immobilized by the magnitude of the disaster confronting them. They then dashed across the yard and disappeared behind the barn, from the main structure of which smoke was already billowing. Inside the house itself a bell began shrilling in further alarm, and a second group of men emerged and followed the first. There was no indication of anybody in command. It was plain that a most satisfactory dis-organization – indeed panic – obtained.

'There's quite a spot of fire-fighting equipment in the furthest shed,' Tim said. 'Quite enough to keep them busy for a time in a more or less rational way. But will they have left a guard behind them? That's the umpteen-dollar question, Uncle Gilbert. A matter of nice psychological calculation, in fact. But we take our chance, don't we? Into the Valley of Death, Colonel Averell. *Come on!'*

For the moment the yard was deserted, the entire force of the enemy being occupied at the back of the barn, where contradictory orders were now being shouted amid what it was to be hoped was still entire confusion. Tongues of flame were beginning to lick through the shingled roof of the building, and at one corner there was a cascade of sparks and the crash of falling timber.

'Too hot, too hot,' Tim yelled wildly, 'I have *tremor cordis* on me!' With his uncle abreast of him, he dashed across the yard to the back door. They bundled themselves through it, and Tim banged it to. 'Bolts,' he shouted, 'splendid bolts!' He rammed them home. 'Just do the same by the front door and any others, and the bloody castle's ours. Wait a minute, though.' He paused and took a deep breath. 'Police!' he bellowed surprisingly. 'Come out, you bastards, in the name of the law!'

There was silence. Tim's voice had echoed as a voice echoes only in an almost void and empty house.

'It may be a castle,' Averell said soberly. 'But it looks as if it's going to be a castle under siege.'

'Too true, Uncle Gilbert. But sufficient unto the day. Stay here. I'll make the next recce.' And – much as he had done at Boxes when under threat from what had proved to be the harmless if vexatious Gustave Flaubert – Tim went off to make a round of the ground floor of the house. Averell moved to a window of the back lobby in which he stood, and found himself looking across at the barn through heavy bars. There were now men in front of the building, directing upon it the jet from a fire-hose that seemed far from adequate to the task in hand. It couldn't be long before they had to give up their endeavours as a bad job. But there was now another factor in the situation. Over the burning building there hung a great plume of smoke which must be visible for miles around. He remembered that a mere disaster to a haystack produced just that effect. What happened in such a case? Did anybody alert the nearest fire-brigade if the owners of the rick failed to do so? It occurred to him that somewhere in this house there must be a telephone, and that he ought to locate it, dial 999, and contact the police. They were more urgently required, it seemed to him, than any number of fire engines. But now Tim had returned, and this possibility was ruled out by the first words he spoke.

'Telephone disconnected,' Tim said. 'These chaps seem to be here in a pretty temporary way. Nothing but camp beds and kitchen furniture. Security so-so. All the lower windows barred or with lattices rigged up on them. But they've only to find a few ladders, and come at us simultaneously through several first-storey windows, and we're sunk all right. So there's no time to waste. Come into the hall.'

The hall was a large affair which one might feel had seen better days, but never very good ones; and up one side of it climbed a pretentious but uncarpeted staircase. Tim went halfway up, stopped, and shouted at the top of his voice.

'Dave – are you there?'

Again there was an echo – and no reply. The silence fell on them dull and ominous.

'Dave, you great oaf – are you there?'

This note of impatience had been sounded in vain. But the silence was not now entire. There were voices from somewhere outside the house. Perhaps the fire-fighters had given up and come back. Perhaps it was only two or three of them, returning on one occasion or another. In either event the issue must be the same. The invaders – or at least the fact of their existence – would be discovered.

'Isn't it likely,' Averell said, 'that Dave will be tied up somewhere – and gagged?'

'Yes, it is – and we must search the whole bloody dump. Let's begin–' Tim broke off.

'But listen!'

From somewhere above their heads there had come a faint call – and it was repeated now. Although faint, it was also angry.

'Tim! Tim you silly sod – up here at the top!'

Tim gave a shout of triumph and bounded up the remainder of the staircase. Without pausing to call out again, he disappeared up a further flight. His uncle followed with what speed he could. When he reached the attic storey it was to find his nephew halted before a stout wooden door at the end of a corridor.

'Dave,' he was calling, 'are you in there?'

'Yes, I damn-well am!' It was plain that Dave was wholesomely enraged. 'And I don't think there's a lock. Simply a couple of hefty bolts.'

'That's it – just an improvised clink for an all-time idiot.' Tim shouted this in a most unamiable manner. It was not the least strange fact about this extraordinary situation – Averell reflected – that the two young men were affecting to be cross with one another. 'You oughtn't to be allowed out by yourself,' Tim shouted for good measure. 'Lucky that nannie had an eye on you.' He drew back the bolts and flung open the door. 'Dr Livingstone, I presume?' he said.

It was a small room lit by an inaccessible skylight, and it contained very little except

Dave himself. Dave wasn't in bonds; he had simply been securely incarcerated. Across the dusty floor his footprints could be distinguished as he had prowled to and fro – like a mangy circus tiger (Tim was to say) in a cage as small as the cruelty to animals people would allow. The furniture consisted of a rickety cane chair and an incongruously massive kitchen table. On the table was a mug, an empty beer can, and the remains of a cold chicken.

'Well, I'm damned,' Tim said. 'Guzzling too.' His conduct as he spoke was at variance with these words, since he had grabbed his friend, hugged him, and was waltzing him round the table. 'No complaints, I suppose? Treated very well? Don't forget you have to say that to the reporters. It's the regular thing.'

'Bugger the reporters – and let's get out. Where are all those chaps?'

'Busy extinguishing a fire started by a careless tramp.'

'I don't know that they are,' Averell said. 'Just listen to that.'

This was an unnecessary injunction, since a great banging had suddenly made itself inescapably audible below.

'It's the back door,' Tim said calmly. 'They can't open it, and it puzzles them. Let them puzzle away while we do a quick think. On just how to fight our way out.'

'There are about a dozen of them,' Dave said with a drop into sobriety. 'I don't want to be discouraging, but it's a ratio of four to one. Mr Averell, did you do unarmed combat back in that Hitler's time?'

'I'm afraid not.'

'Then we'd better arm ourselves. Tim, what do you think about that table? Could we get the legs off it? They'd make very handy clubs, and the joints feel a bit wonky.'

The young men at once applied themselves to this project with vigour, upending the table and wrenching at the legs with a will. They came away quite easily.

'Bags I this one,' Tim said childishly. 'It has a couple of usefully nasty nails left in it.' He brandished it in air. 'And now we'd better nip downstairs and see if we can simply make a run for it. That would be simplest, of course, in the circumstances. But I rather reckon that battle it will have to be.'

'I wonder about simply sticking to the defensive?' Averell asked. 'I can't believe that a fire like that is going to be ignored. Quite soon the police are bound to turn up, and these crooks know it. I doubt whether, as things are, they'd see much point in making an assault on us. Their booty has gone for good, and their captive is out of their grasp. What they must be thinking of at this moment is calling it a day and making themselves scarce.'

These were highly rational thoughts, which were respectfully listened to. But their basis was now promptly falsified in a dramatic manner. The hammering at the back door had ceased, but only to be replaced by fresh manifestations of violence. Through the house reverberated a crash of breaking glass – oddly accompanied by the roar, abruptly silenced, of some powerful engine.

'They've got out a tractor or something,' Tim said, 'and smashed their way in. Just the idea I had with that potty little motor-mower. Too late to nip quietly out, chums. It's the siege, all right. They know we're in the house – or that somebody's in the house, because otherwise that back door couldn't have been bolted against them. So they'll start hunting round at once.'

'No bloody bolts up here,' Dave said. 'Or not on the inside of this door. Could we get on the roof? If we could, and if there aren't too many trapdoors and fire-escapes to it, we could hold out for quite a time. Like those chaps who start rioting in gaols.'

'Let's get into the corridor and see.' Tim had moved rapidly to the door. 'I could reach an affair of that sort by standing on your hulking great shoulders. And we could haul up Uncle Gilbert by his braces.' Tim flung the door open, and then as abruptly banged it shut again. 'No go,' he said. 'They're on the floor beneath us, and will be up here in a jiffy. Listen to them! It's like a whole blasted battalion. Prepare to sell your lives dearly. But perhaps they'll only beat us up in a savage and vengeful manner before making tracks from the place.'

Averell found this hopeful thought not particularly comforting. There was now a great deal of noise immediately below, compounded by angry shouting, slamming doors, and the pounding of heavy feet.

'No good trying to barricade this door,' Dave said. 'There's nothing but the remains of that rotten table.'

'Not the drill, anyway,' Tim said. 'Much too passive. You and I just stand on either side of it, and swat them in turn as they come in. Think of them as cockroaches or something. Uncle Gilbert will simply stand by and give an additional bash to any of them that looks like requiring it. Here they come! Stand by.'

Composedly the two young men took up this suggested station on either side of the door. They might have been tennis players positioning themselves at the start of a game. Then each poised his table leg in air – with Tim being careful to orient his two nasty nails to the most potentially lacerating effect. It was a grotesque spectacle – like a farcical episode in some brutal knock-about film in a past age. And now there were running footsteps, a sharp command, heavy breathing, immediately outside. The door flew open. The young men tautened their arms.

'Stop!' Averell shouted.

He was just in time. It was policemen who were tumbling into the attic room.

21

It was the police helicopter that had shattered the windows. You can land a helicopter on a handkerchief, but it is usual not to come too near expanses of glass. As the forces of the law, however, had been equipped to storm the house through its first-floor windows, the havoc wrought by this particular machine had come in quite handy as speeding up the operation, which in fact was all over in under fifteen minutes. The police, indeed, had been a little disconcerted at finding no criminals inside the house, and had achieved much hurried ferreting about and vain rummaging. But eventually the whole lot had been rounded up in the outbuildings and the yard, and were now being ushered into several capacious black vehicles. Most of them being covered in soot and ashes from their vain fire-fighting, they presented a somewhat woebegone spectacle. Their demeanour, however, was in the main philosophic. Police brutality (for which Tim was keeping an eye wide open) could not honestly be said to be occurring.

Police curiosity was another matter. The Inspector in charge of the operation was under the irritating persuasion that it was his business to ask questions rather than answer them. Tim in the future was always to refer to this final half-hour of the adventure as 'our interrogation' or 'when we were bloody-helping the fuzz with their inquiries'. For a time, indeed, Averell was afraid that the two young men were going to prove positively truculent; that they were about to express themselves as disgusted that a private-enterprise Operation had been crassly blundered in upon just when all was going swimmingly. But this fear proved baseless, since it failed to take account of that sense of fair play which has been whacked into all nicely brought up English boys. Tim and Dave (not to speak of Uncle Gilbert) had been rescued, and they knew it. Tim even managed to utter some embarrassed words to this effect. These were well received.

Dave gave an account of himself. Dozing down the street, he'd actually given that lot a casual hand at loading up the stuff they'd then smuggled into the house in Uffington Street as band paraphernalia. When he'd got the implications of this clear in his head he'd gone to do a look-see, and had later decided to confer with Tim. But then the bastards had jumped out of nowhere and clobbered him.

'Not,' Dave said magnanimously, 'that

they weren't quite decent once they got me out of the bloody crate. Fed me, and even treated me to some tinned stuff passing as beer.'

'It's not precisely a major point in their favour,' the Inspector said dryly. 'Did they say anything about holding you to ransom?'

'No, they did not. They weren't exactly chatty, you know.'

'Did you yourself reflect that something of the sort might have become their main interest in you?'

'It did cross my mind.'

'Would you describe yourself as rather a notable prize for people thinking of that line of business?'

'I don't know at all. I suppose my people are fairly well off. As people go, that is.'

'Thank you very much.' The Inspector spoke rather as if dropping this reasonably comprehensible young man into a pigeon-hole from which he could be retrieved at need. 'I don't think I have anything more to ask you at present.'

'But I've something to ask *you*,' Dave said – now a shade belligerently. 'Would you mind telling me how your people got on to the thing?'

'Oh, not in the least.' The Inspector appeared delighted. 'We have been acting on information received.'

'Who from?'

'Ah, that's another matter.'

'Damn it all–'

'My dear young man, the reply I have given you would satisfy any judge in the High Court, and it will have to satisfy you.' The Inspector smiled at Dave in the friendliest way, much as if he had taken a liking to him in a totally non-fuzzlike manner. 'And now I have one or two questions to put to Mr Barcroft.'

'Fire ahead,' Tim said grimly. 'But I don't undertake to answer them, and am not obliged to do so.'

'Of course not. But what I have in mind is merely something that needn't embarrass you in the slightest degree. I'm just curious about the origin of that fire.'

'Oh,' Tim said – and for a moment seemed to have been put decidedly at a stand. Then he took a deep breath. 'There was this tramp, you see. Your men must have spotted him.'

'I'm not aware that my men spotted any tramp, Mr Barcroft.'

'Good lord! For how long have you had this place under observation, Inspector?'

'Since noon.'

'Under *close* observation?'

'Certainly.'

'Everything tied up, and even the guard dogs taken care of?'

'All appropriate measures were put into operation.'

'Then it's very odd you don't know about the tramp.'

'It is – decidedly.'

'A bloody careless tramp. He went into the shed to light a fag. And he must–'

'No doubt he must.' The Inspector was staring hard at Tim. 'Would you be able to identify him?'

'I'm sure I could identify him. And my uncle could probably identify him too. Isn't that right, Uncle–' Tim paused fractionally. 'Isn't that right, Uncle Georges?'

Averell was momentarily confounded by this, which he took to be one of his nephew's most atrocious pieces of mischief, and decidedly untimely at that. But the Inspector was looking at him expectantly.

'Well,' Averell said, 'he seemed to me a fairly ordinary tramp, although no doubt careless beyond the average. But – do you know? – I rather thought he had a cast in one eye.'

'That's it!' Tim said – and immediately touched sublimity. 'Or was it a limp, *mon oncle?* I can't really remember.'

The Inspector breathed a shade heavily, and for a moment affected to consult an unused notebook in front of him.

'You know,' he asked Tim, 'just what that barn contained?'

'Rubbish out of the bank, I suppose. I don't much mind what it contained myself.

No doubt the bank people won't be too pleased.'

'But you are pleased, Mr Barcroft, that you got into this house in the endeavour to rescue your friend?'

'I bloody well am.'

'Then I think that is all.' The Inspector closed his notebook in what might have been termed a symbolic fashion. 'And it is not my impression that we shall get far in the hunt for that tramp. He will prove, I imagine, rather carelessly, to have lost himself.' The Inspector looked straight at Tim. 'But you needn't let that disturb you.'

Tim was silent for a moment, and then spoke four memorable words.

'Thank you very much.'

On the sweep outside the Black Marias of the law were preparing to depart. So was the helicopter. The show was over. But suddenly the Inspector appeared to bethink himself.

'There are just one or two formalities,' he said. 'Of identification chiefly.' He turned to Gilbert Averell. 'Would you, sir, happen to have any present means of identifying yourself?'

It was the moment of truth. There was nothing to do but to rise to it. Averell produced from an inner pocket the passport of the Prince de Silistrie and handed it to the inquisitor in front of him. The Inspector opened it, studied it for a moment only, and then handed it back.

'Thank you, Prince, he said politely. It was as if he regarded it as the most natural thing in the world that a well-bred youth such as Mr Barcroft should run to a French uncle of exalted rank. 'May I ask if you intend to stay long in England?'

'Only over the next two or three days,' Averell said firmly. And he added, 'Might I be required to return for the purpose of giving evidence against those criminals?'

'Possibly. Yes, possibly.'

'I could be required to do so?'

'Dear me, no – and indeed there may be no necessity for your presence. And no English court could require the attendance, simply for the purpose of giving testimony, of any foreign national.' The Inspector glanced at Averell whimsically. 'We could hardly start extradition proceedings, could we?'

'*Merci, Monsieur l'Inspecteur,*' Gilbert Averell said. And he managed a dignified Gallic bow.

They drove back to London in Dave's car, and had reached the motorway before Tim spoke.

'Quite a decent chap,' Tim said, and paused. 'But a bit thick, as they all are,' he added complacently. 'Couldn't spot the fact, Uncle Gilbert, that you're no more a Frog prince than I am.'

'What you are,' Dave said cheerfully to his friend, 'is an all-time silly sod. I say! Where shall we go for dinner?'

EPILOGUE

IN FRANCE

'My dear friend,' the Prince de Silistrie said, 'I hope you had an enjoyable vacation?'

'Yes, indeed. Decidedly.'

'And I too. I visited the tombs of the Etruscans. Gilbert Averell visited the tombs of the Etruscans, ought I not to say? Melancholy, those *mellone* – but by fortune less extensive than the later catacombs of our own most holy religion.' The Prince de Silistrie, who was a very devout man, paused becomingly on this. 'Yet how joyous a people, Gilbert! The little statues – *figurines*, as you also say – dancing, diving, running, and sometimes so shamelessly Priapic, in such readiness, as they pursue, it must be, the nymphs! Your great writer David H Lawrence celebrates this?

'I suppose he does,' Averell said, and glanced a shade uneasily at his friend. The two men were lunching at Poissy, and the Seine sparkled in May sunshine round the little island on which their restaurant lay. Many gentlemen were already in straw hats. It was all very Monet, very Renoir – or Lambinet, Averell thought, recalling his favourite novel by Henry James. They were both silent for a moment: two brothers quietly enjoying one another's company, as they must appear

251

to any casual regard. 'And you had no difficulty with the passport?' Averell asked cautiously.

'None whatever. And how I acted one of your admired compatriots! At Volterra, in the *Porcellino* – so charming a name for a little hostelry – I breakfast on the bacon and eggs. Think of that, my friend!'

'And *l'estomac* stood up to it well? Always in France one considers *l'estomac*.'

'Indeed, yes.' Georges signalled no disapproval of this pleasantry. 'Only when I returned to Paris there was an incident. *C'est le curieux de l'affaire*. I received a photograph. "Snapshot" is perhaps the proper term.'

'A snapshot of just what?' Averell asked – although he knew perfectly well.

'Of myself – or such was the suggestion – ravishing an English rose. In a grotto, or some such secluded place. It is a fresh light upon your character, my dear Gilbert. I hope the little *rencontre* went well. English roses are said to be so chilly, are they not? It is as if the dew were upon them always.'

'That is complete nonsense.'

'They are, in fact, ardent? It is a calumny?'

'I'm not talking about that. I mean about what was taking place. I was comforting an innocent girl, little more than a child, who happened to be very much upset.'

'I am disappointed.'

'There was a confounded spy. He thought

he was on your trail, as a matter of fact.'

'Quite so. You must forgive the jest. It was Minette who was his paymistress. "Paymistress" is allowed?'

'I suppose so. But the word is not in common use.'

'Thank you, Gilbert. I note the fact. But yes, it was *la belle Minette*. So jealous, and so rich as well! It is a dangerous combination, that.'

'If I have got you into trouble with a mistress – "Pay" or otherwise – I apologize.'

'*N'importe*. Minette and I, we shall laugh over it together yet.' And the Prince de Silistrie raised a hand in the air.

'*Garcon,*' he called out, '*deux fines!*'

The brandy arrived, and over raised glasses a solemn attestation of unflawed friendship ensued.

The publishers hope that this book has given you enjoyable reading. Large Print Books are especially designed to be as easy to see and hold as possible. If you wish a complete list of our books please ask at your local library or write directly to:

Dales Large Print Books
Magna House, Long Preston,
Skipton, North Yorkshire.
BD23 4ND